SAXON

ANNALISE ALEXIS

CHAPTER ONE

Leigh

Twenty minutes. That's all I have until this beautiful beast makes or breaks my career. I'm either going down in history as the first female to design a sub capable of taking a human to the bottom of the New Mariana Trench, or as an obsessed, ice queen with a hard-on for failure.

Let's hope it's not door number two.

The comfortable chatter of my crew in my earpiece helps to settle the frantic beat of my heart. Normally, they get on my nerves. Especially Johan because he never shuts up. But right now it's dampening the back and forth I'm having with my inner bitch.

Even with the noise, she won't let me forget how much is riding on this test dive. What has it been? Six years? I've missed holidays and nights out with the girls, thrown away countless relationships for this exact moment, and I'm either going to throw up or scream.

If this baby crumples under the pressure, I'm done for. My job, my dreams, and the meager credibility I've managed to build will be laid to rest at the bottom of the ocean.

"Hold her steady now, boss. You're almost there," Johan, my sub team captain, says. I'm sure the rest of the crew's on pins and needles watching the live feed from the boat. I spent years being on that side of the action and damn, if it doesn't feel good to finally be in the captain's chair.

"Are you getting good feedback from the exterior cameras? You know Elgin will throw a fit if I don't get quality images tomorrow," I say, salivating like one of Pavlov's dogs at the idea of tomorrow's maiden dive. To be the first human to explore the deepest depths known to man? And in a sub I championed, no less? Talk about girl boner. It's the things dreams are made of.

"Looking good from here. The still image cameras are working seamlessly, as well as the 3D. And before you ask, yes the battery management system is operating smoothly as well. They're all doing exactly what we created them to do."

The gauge on my onboard computer system moves, the fathometer dinging every time the craft descends another thousand feet. Call it superstitious, but I designed it that way—like a mother listening to her newborn breathe, I need to hear my baby. Need to make sure she doesn't crash and burn like the last one.

I just need to make it to thirty-two thousand feet before I can bring her back and declare her dive ready to descend the additional five thousand feet to the underwater caves tomorrow.

She's tough as diamonds and slim enough to fit the second smallest crevice in the newly found portion of the trench. With state-of-the-art imaging and temperature sensors, I can get readings that no one else has ever gotten. The exact temperature and chemical makeup of the lowest point on the planet, maybe even a clue as to how a series of caves formed down there to begin with.

Damn, just the idea of that kind of data gives me the tingles —and they said nothing was better than sex.

Focusing on the positive, I try to ignore the doubt creeping in. I'm still descending. It was at this moment, near thirty-one thousand feet, the Juniper sank. When I failed, I nearly lost everything.

My math was wrong. The pressure per square inch was greater than I'd calculated, the temperature colder, and the Juniper sank on its unmanned test mission.

I lost all confidence and nearly quit. The only way I could even keep my job was to accept a giant pay cut and turn a blind eye to Elgin taking an axe to my funding. It was total humiliation. There were endless news articles about how I crashed and burned, but after spending six days in a bottle of rum, I got myself together and tried again.

This time will be different. I spent the prime of my thirties creating this magnificent bitch and there's no way I'm failing this time.

She's going to make it, and then I'm going to finally get the credit I deserve.

After the Great Shift in 2045, an earthquake that nearly tore the Pacific Ocean in half, the seabed split, revealing several underground tunnels and caverns that were deeper and more complex than anything previously explored. So much so, everyone said it couldn't be done.

But the newly revealed network of passages isn't impossible to navigate. It just needs a machine capable of surviving it.

I tighten my grip on the controls and hold my breath, trying to channel all the power of my female ancestors, dance a little jig, cross my fingers, and do whatever-the-hell else I have to in order to make this happen.

"Holy crap, we're almost there," Johan screeches, and I cringe at the feedback in my ear. As Henrietta, my sub, hits the lowest previously recorded depth, my anticipation doubles. The computer dings, and cheers erupt back at the lab.

I can't help but laugh as my lungs start to deflate and some of the tension leaves me. For once, I'm going to let myself enjoy this moment. I deserve it. And after tomorrow, the world will see what Dr. Leigh Lennox is capable of.

The entire ascent feels surreal. I'm finally on the cusp of achieving my dreams. Maybe, after this, whatever black cloud has been following me around will die a merciless death, and I'll be accepted back into all the scientific circles that laughed me out before.

No, screw that. I'm going to make my own damn circle. And I'm not letting any of those old, pale, dickheads in.

AS SOON AS I get safely back on deck, my crew's there to greet me, several of them with drinks in hand. They're all fully dressed. Even Rafe who normally sports a wrinkled v-neck and last week's jeans looks like he's showered.

"Whoa, what'd I miss?" I ask, accepting a schooner of beer from Johan. Normally, we don't bring alcohol on the boat, but today's test dive was definitely a special occasion.

"He looks good, right?" Risa, my robotics girl, says jerking her chin at Rafe. He turns the color of beet soup and Johan elbows him in the side. Risa smiles and clanks her glass against mine. "You better go get dressed. It's going to be here any minute now."

"What is?"

"When Elgin got the relay data from the test dive, he practically jumped for joy. He was so happy he arranged a party yacht for us tonight. The entire crew's invited."

My drink nearly slips out of my hand. "Seriously?"

Risa nods, and I throw back the rest of my beer. The excitement and relief I felt just seconds before sours a little. There's no way Elgin can afford to sign off on a purchase of that magnitude. Either we aren't as strapped as I think we are, or he's single handedly been blocking most of my funding requests for the past year and a half. I haven't said anything about it out of fear of retaliation. We hardly have anything left. So, whose money is he using?

Making a beeline for my room, I rip off my clothes and hop in the shower. The water pressure on Daxx Corp's research vessel sucks, but it's got enough cabins for me and the rest of the crew and a launch pad for Henrietta. Not two seconds after I've stepped under the spray, my work phone rings.

Elgin starts talking before I've even managed to put the phone to my ear. "I hear congratulations are in order. Did you receive my little gift?" he asks.

"Everyone told me about the yacht, if that's what you're referring to."

He laughs in that elitist, douchey kind of way. "It is, it is. Hey, while I've got you on the phone, I'd like to go over a few of the changes I've made for the launch day schedule."

Changes. I've. Made.

"I thought we'd gone over this a million times. The launch is scheduled for tomorrow night. You can't just change things at the last second."

"Sure I can. I'm the boss, right? After putting a lot of thought into it, I've decided I'm going to be the one to go down."

Several long seconds go by, and I still can't find words to

respond to him that consist of more than four letters and aren't preceded by the words "you" and "slimy."

"What? I must have misheard you because—"

"You didn't. I'm taking your place."

My tongue feels like sandpaper against the roof of my mouth. "No. I've waited my whole life for an opportunity like this. You can't just—"

"I can. It's already arranged. Come tomorrow night, you will be alongside your team in the lab where you belong, and I will take the Nautilus Five down."

"The hell you will. That maiden dive is mine."

"*Was* yours."

The walls close in, and I can't get enough air. I'm so pissed I'm shaking. "Elgin, don't do this."

He laughs. "Begging doesn't suit you, Dr. Lennox. If I were you, I'd enjoy yourself tonight. I have it on good authority that Daxx Corp will be pursuing different ventures after this, and I suspect your services will no longer be needed."

Phone in hand, I stand there naked for several minutes after he hangs up. Did I just get fired? Did that megalomaniac really just say he was going to take the maiden dive in the sub I created and steal my chance at being the first to explore the trench?

Fuck that. And fuck him.

You want to know what you don't do? Fire a girl and then tell her she can't do something. Why? Because she has nothing to lose.

I've worked my butt off for more than half a decade on Henrietta, and he isn't going to take the opportunity from me. No one, and I mean, no one but me will be the first down there.

Opting for sweats rather than the semi-dressy attire everyone else seemed to be planning on, I throw my wet hair up in a messy bun and shuffle out my door and onto the deck.

Risa cocks a brow and scurries over while the rest of the crew heads for the party yacht. "You okay? You look like someone just ran over your puppy."

They did. Except, it wasn't a dog. It was my life's work—and my livelihood to boot.

I force my lips into a smile. "No, nothing like that. Just tired. I think I'm going to hit the sack early to prep for tomorrow."

She tips her head to the side and pouts. "You want me to stay here? I could pop open some wine and we could talk about girl stuff."

Gross. I'd rather get a yeast infection than talk about my feelings. Extreme, I know, but it's the truth. Interacting with my cat, Binky, is as far as my social tolerance goes.

"I'm good. Promise. Go have fun!"

I wave as the last of my crew files onto the overpriced boat. I know everyone who comes off and on this vessel, and when I scan each of the faces, I can tell the only person left is Carlos, one of the guys who usually captains the boat. After dropping anchor, he'll be drunk as a skunk all night.

As the laughter of my crew fades and the rumble of the yacht's engine disappears, I grab the unopened beers Johan left on the deck and settle back against the rail.

The rest of my crew won't be back until late afternoon tomorrow, and tonight, I'm going to take what's mine, consequences be damned.

THE SMOOTH STRAPS of my harness fit snugly against my chest, like Henrietta herself is trying to soothe my nerves. Releasing her and getting her in the water alone was tasking, but the automated system Johan helped create made it a breeze compared to how it used to be.

Thank goodness for mandatory training videos. They might have been a total snoozefest, but I wouldn't have known how to operate the controls without them.

"Good girl," I say, patting the front console and giving the pink shark bobblehead above the control yoke a little tap. Stella's fake plastic hips swivel in a red and white hula skirt. A Christmas gift from my niece when she was six, it's been my good luck token ever since. It might be ten years old, but the oversized coconut-covered cleavage and chipped guitar give me endless comfort because they remind me of my niece.

It's been years since I've seen or heard from my sister, and I'm hoping this year that will change. If I can succeed here, I can finally spend some time fixing what my unwavering ambition has broken.

Dressed in nothing but a wetsuit, fuzzy socks, and tennis shoes, I turn on the tiny music player I brought along. Mozart's "Requiem in D Minor" fills the air. The added weight was totally worth the cost.

The music makes Henrietta my personal little happy place, and I try to keep the possibility of failure—and my death— shoved to the back of my mind. My mother taught me to trust myself, if nothing else.

Readying the controls, I flip on the internal recorder but make sure no external signals will be sent. If I can pull this off, Daxx Corp, Elgin, and his boss Sterling will be none the wiser. My little voyage will remain secret, but I can still document it. I can always flip the transmitter on if something goes wrong. It'll automatically connect with the lab.

I refuse to share this moment. Elgin can have the honor of taking the first samples, smiling pretty for the cameras, and all that jazz. I don't really care. It will still be my name on the reports. I created Henrietta. For me, what's important is being the first to see the unseen, something the masses—even my own sister—said I never would.

Achieving this would prove all the loneliness was worth it and that my devotion isn't a baseless obsession.

My heart threatens to jump out of my chest the further we drop. Unable to resist, I've spent most of the past half hour staring out the small window, absorbing every single second. It's so beautiful.

Before I started the dive, the setting sun still streamed through the water, creating the most beguiling patterns of light. With the increased depth came solitude and now, at nine-thousand meters, all I can see is what's on the sonar and the small amount of water illuminated by the external lights.

The pressure gauges beep, announcing that we've hit fourteen thousand pounds per square inch of pressure—enough to crush most ocean equipment. This is what kept people from reaching the bottom of the trench—the Challenger Deep— in the early years.

Here we go. The entrance to where the earthquake deepened the trench is close.

My lungs tighten, and I swallow down a sudden rush of panic as the pressure nears sixteen-thousand pounds. "Come on, Henrietta. You can do this, baby. You're literally made for this, girl."

The external lights dim in the murky water as we break the second-to-last boundary to have been crossed. "Ha! Hell yes, girl. Go! We can do this," I yell, grabbing my bobblehead to give her a big kiss. "Stella, you big beautiful slut, we're doing it!" Turning her around so her lopsided googly eyes can see the depths she helped me reach, I wiggle in excitement.

The fathometer registers the depth again. Sixty meters from the record descent, and I stare at the numbers as they grow larger and larger until we're five meters away.

My heart skips a beat—or ten—the years of depression and failure flashing through my mind as we slide into the undocumented and unknown. My tears fall. Big fat drops of success pour down my face, and I let the moment consume me as Debussy plays in the background.

I did it. I really freaking did it. The elation—the satisfaction—is just as wonderful as I imagined. Screw every person who ever said I was too blond to be an engineer, too soft to work in the private sector and survive, and too, well...*everything* to convince someone to finance me.

Screw being too loud, too opinionated, and thinking too far outside the box. I'm the first damn human, woman no less, to breach the barrier and enter the only unexplored place on the planet. Take that all you naysaying negative Nancies!

The hull whines slightly, adjusting to the increased pressure, and I glance over the latest mapping coordinates and compare them with the data I calculated this morning. Everything's the same. Water temp, pressure, density all seem to be within the expected parameters.

"All right, baby. I'm letting you drive. Show me what you can do," I say, engaging the auto-drive. Henrietta scans ten feet in every direction, trying to maintain a safe zone to prevent collisions with the piles of earth and rock around us.

The silt hangs heavy this deep, making it difficult to see, and the lights are pretty much pointless, so I turn them off. Anything down here hasn't ever been exposed to the light, and there's no way I'm going to see anything bioluminescent with them on.

That's the beauty of Henrietta. I can't see in the dark, but she can. Switching to the enhanced night vision, I watch as she lowers us into the widest cavern on the right. It's our best shot to explore.

There's nothing for several minutes, just an inky blackness and the surrounding rocks, and for a second, I start to second guess myself. It's so dark and so quiet, save for the light hum of Chopin coming through the speaker, and no one else knows I'm here.

I only wish I could have told my best friend, Anya. But with her psych issues—and all the people and governments she thinks are after her—she can't afford it. She doesn't know how to keep herself out of trouble, and if I can avoid getting her involved, I will.

My own selfish choices lost me my family once. I won't make the same mistake again. Henrietta leans a full ninety degrees to navigate a sharp right, and I bite my lip, trying to ignore how unnatural it feels to be turned on my side. Luckily, the straps were made for this kind of movement so I don't slide an inch, but poor Stella goes tits over ass and smacks into the back wall.

A cold hollowness climbs up my throat as she turns an additional ten degrees, and I close my eyes, trying to center myself before I puke. But thoughts of Mister Fancy Pants, Elgin, sitting in this chair bring me right out of the panic.

I wish I could be there for that. *I wish I could be there for everything.* Maybe I can bribe Risa to use the internal cameras to take still shots of his twisted face when Henrietta dances like this with him in the chair.

The last Chopin track ends, and when Henrietta rights herself, Stella comes rolling back and I reset the music. There's something about a soft orchestra that soothes me and a badass one that gets my adrenaline pumping. Classical is so underrated. I swear, it was the original metal.

As the melody begins to play, I return my gaze to the sonar

screen. Or try to. Instead, I'm drawn to the view window by what looks like tiny green lights. There are no words to describe it. Little glowing organisms float freely through the cave, illuminating it enough for me to see the enclosed space, and I stare with child-like wonder.

I don't care what will happen if Elgin finds out I did this. This is so worth it.

No more than fifty-feet across, this section of tunnel leads to the mouth of a larger cave. Once we make it in, I have to unstrap my harness and smash my face against the window.

"Holy crap on a cracker, Stella, this is unheard of..." The words slip out in a breathy rush as I struggle to believe what I'm seeing.

Large clusters of bioluminescent plant life grow from the walls like some kind of multi-colored carpet, and schools of those tiny green floaters swim by. Using Henrietta's arm to snag a few, I zoom in with the camera.

Holy shit. There's something resting on the sea floor. It's large. Around twelve feet in length. And wait? Are there more of them?

The shiny exterior would lead me to believe it's some kind of metal, but down here? How's that even possible? And if it is...how is it withstanding all this pressure?

With only two feet of its silver cone-shaped top protruding, I can't really get a good view of what it is. Years of growth obscures the design that peeks out near the tip. Whatever it is, I'm drawn to it, and the urge to horde it like a dragon with treasure is nearly too much to resist. Leaving it here for Elgin to find is going to kill me.

I want whatever this is to be mine. I *need* it to be mine.

My heart's pounding, and my fingertips itch to touch it. Not smart considering I'm miles below sea level and would pop like a pimple if I opened Henrietta's door.

Could this be some kind of ancient artifact? Oh, holy balls! Did I discover some kind of dead city or civilization?

Ugh, I can't see anything. I need to get closer...

Turning off the auto-drive, I switch on the lights so I can maneuver Henrietta's retrieval arm to take samples of the cave wall. Maybe I can clear off some of the debris to better identify whatever this is.

Trying to be as careful as I can, I move the control only a fraction of an inch—paying close attention to Henrietta's safe boundaries on the view screen. I extend her arm with the flip of a switch and use it to collect a few samples from the top, near where the thick build up begins. It's harder than I expect but, with a little more strength, I manage to wipe a foot long portion of debris clear and wait for the silt to settle.

Movement flickers out of the corner of my eye, and I lean closer to the window, trying to see through the sludge I sent flying everywhere. What the hell is that?

Not willing to blink and miss a single second, I grab the main control arm to move Henrietta closer. She starts to yell at me, the bright yellow blinking light on the screen warning me I'm closer to the wall than she wants me to be.

I'm still two feet away. We're fine. I just need to get a little closer.

With my face still pressed to the glass like it will actually help, I guide us in farther, gripping the controls so tightly my fingers turn white. My life literally depends on my control right now.

Focusing on a thickened area the gap in the debris reveals, I catch sight of a weird shadow. Is that something I'm creating?

Oh, fuck! A squid-like creature clinging to the silver object's tiny window swims away, and I jump back, yanking on the controls and sending us crashing into the far wall of the cave. I'm thrown forward by the collision. Pain radiates across my scalp, and Henrietta's alarms are screaming, but I can't move to answer them. The room spins, and a heavy weight pulls me under.

CHAPTER TWO

Saxon

Mine.

Danger.

The urge to protect stirs me from sleep, but I cannot move more than a hand to reach her. *Wake, you stupid bastard, wake!* The stasis-inducing serum running through my veins stifles my attempts, but her call sends me reeling toward consciousness. I cannot scent her. Cannot see her. It is as if my eyes have gone blind, but I feel her closeness and her desperate need for me. My female is dying. And I do not even know her name.

A jolt of pain settles in my abdomen where my heart lies, and my claws extend. No. I will not lose the one I have been searching my entire existence for to a stupid travel chamber. My brethren. Maybe they can help.

The communicator in my wrist that connects us flickers, showing the existence of three other Revari pods, but the activator is dead. Like mine, their pods must not be fully operational or we would have been alerted to the error. Shit. I cannot reach them.

Ripping the injection tubes from the bundle of veins in my arm, I test each limb quickly, shaking them awake before I throw myself out of the padded mold that's held me for the duration of my slumber. I do not know how long I have been in stasis, or where it is that I have landed, but none of that matters. Only her. Forever her.

The waning connection between us screams at me—stimulating my drive to protect, to comfort, to heal. I press my hand to my pod wall, activating the internal controls to open the hatch, but it refuses. Its sensors are breaking down the components of the substance surrounding me and it continues to deny my exit, why! Cursed chamber! I do not care if it is safe!

The environment beyond my pod is harsh with very little gas to filter through my lungs and only meets the minimal life requirement parameters.

Sinking the sharp edges of my teeth into my hand, I ignore the pain, smear the life blood required to override the lock, and burst through the hatch—my pod propelling itself up as I exit. Pure agony folds me in half. Crushing pressure on all sides bears down, forcing my shape to shift, my bones to soften, but I do not slow. Not even the unfamiliar darkness and violent wet ooze can stop me from freeing my mate. From saving her.

The sound of the aquatic beasts around me register, and I emulate them, using their pitch to aid my weakened vision. The echoes and our connection guiding me, I find the rough edges of some kind of craft. My mate is inside, but I can find no way in.

I rage against it, but the intense pressure prevents me from exerting my true strength.

My female's heart beats rapidly, and with the wet ooze filling my ears, it is dangerously faint. I must get her away from this place. With my primary breathing passages unable to filter the ooze, only the ancillary passages behind my ears and nostrils allow me to dissolve and absorb the elements.

I cannot survive like this for long, and I fear this environment will not be sustainable for her either. The ancient sky spirits cannot have her yet. She is mine.

Panic courses through me, stoking something I long thought dead, and with a muted roar, I propel the craft up through a narrowed set of tunnels. The faster I go, the more her heart weakens. Fuck. I do not understand this.

The pressure. My own body is struggling to adjust. Perhaps hers is having difficulty also.

I raise the craft until her heart rate slows again, then wait for it to regulate before I push the craft up even more.

She's losing too much blood. This is taking too long.

The pressures lessens, and light from a crescent shaped moon illuminates the wet ooze. Muscles weakening, driven solely by rage and a primal desire to feel the warmth of my mate beneath me, I bring her to the surface and scan for a solid mass to lay her on.

The nearest land mass is too far. She will not make it, but a bulky craft hovers on the surface nearby.

I must release her from her vessel. I must save her. She is to become my world. I cannot let her perish before I have the chance to show her what she will be to me. And what I am meant to be for her.

The walls of the vessel are strong, and the hatch is secured, but it is no match for my determination. Ripping through the hinges, I lunge in, wary of that damned wet ooze filling the chamber.

Get back, you foul, filthy bastard.

Pulling my female into my arms just as the destroyed craft

sinks below the surface, I ensure her breathing passages remain dry.

Careful not to crush her delicate form, I fight through the wet ooze to the craft and climb on. Her temperature is too low, her heart weakened, but as I cradle her and warm her with my own heat, the most beguiling pink tinge blooms on her cheeks.

She is more beautiful than I could have ever dreamed.

The large gash in her scalp begins to stream red again, and I lay her down to rip into my own skin, using the clotting properties my life blood contains to seal her wound.

Signs of life stir inside the strange craft, and I roar, extending my claws, prepared to destroy whatever else threatens my female. There are more scents than I can count and all are unfamiliar. A furry creature advances, back raised in aggression, and expels a hiss. Its message is clear. It believes this female is hers.

Tiny creature, you cannot have her.

Baring my teeth, I emulate its warning shriek, and it hops up and scurries back to a large room in the middle of the craft. My female reaches out, eyes still heavy with sleep, but finds nothing but air. I long to answer her touch, but I do not wish to scare her.

"Binky? Where...are...you?"

Her words... I cannot understand them. Why? The language simulator in my brain should analyze the sounds, creating a construct of her language. The skin has overgrown, but the device still remains near the surface. This implant allots for what? A hundred thousand sun cycles before it requires a reboot? Where the hell did that blackhole spit us out? And when? I must have been in stasis longer than expected.

Gouging the simulator from my flesh, I press the release button and restart the processor like Pavil showed me once before, then shove it back into the wound before it starts to heal.

I have to speak to my female. To hear and understand her needs so that I can meet them.

She drags her hands across the rough flooring. "You furry little twat...how'd you sneak inside Henrietta? Come here and let me snuggle you. I had too much booze. I feel like balls."

Unable to keep my distance, I'm drawn forward. Her scent wraps around me, down to my cock, and I yearn to feel her. Instead I lower my head, letting her hand meet my long black hair. If she wishes to caress the tiny beast that roams this floating fortress, then perhaps this will give her some comfort.

Her hand freezes, and her eyes struggle to open. "What the hell, Bink? Did you get in the butter again? Wait a second...you can't be in Henrietta. Where am I?"

My implant starts to buzz as it processes her words.

Bink. The furry beast has a name.

A deep gasp tears from her throat as her eyes jerk wide, and my female—my mate—struggles to get away from me. Sharp pain tears through my chest, worse than any blade from any foe I have battled. I have waited for this moment, traveled the constellations to find her, and she fears me.

CHAPTER THREE

Leigh

"Oh, holy shit!" I scream and scramble back away from a strange man I was *petting*. A fiery pain radiates across my palms when the rough grip on the deck scrapes against my skin.

The man's head is down, bowed low, and his muscular shoulders are wound tight like he's afraid to move. I can't make out a whole lot under the crappy deck lighting, but I can tell he's *huge*. I'm a good five-feet eleven, and even crouched down, he towers over me. "What do you want? How'd you get on my boat?"

And where is everybody?

"I...do not whiissh to hurt you," he whispers, face still covered with long strands of inky black shoulder-length hair. A salt-infused breeze tickles my face, bringing with it the most incredible smell. Like shooting stars and fresh rain, it pours off of him and surrounds me like a wall of smoke, settling the panic deep in my chest.

"Says the strange man who magically appeared on my boat

in the middle of the Pacific Ocean. Just stay back, or I'll..." *What will you do, Leigh? Insult him to death?* "Well, I don't know what the hell I'll do, but you won't like it!"

"Of course, *Mu Xitall.* I will maintain my distance."

Mu Xitall? What language is that? The closest land masses are the Mariana Islands, and that's definitely not English or Chamorro. Dragging my feet under me in one not-so-swift movement, I tumble forward and prepare to hit the ground, but don't. Strong, *hot* hands grasp my wrists, keeping me upright.

Oh, my crab cakes. He's *touching* me and when he stands to full height, easing me up with him like my thick curves are feather light, whatever words were dangling on the tip of my tongue flee.

Deep golden eyes the color of sunflowers in summer pierce a veil of midnight black hair and stare into mine, glowing beyond the light's reach. My breath stills, lodged in my chest, and I'm so caught up in the moment I forget to be afraid.

"*Your eyes...*" The words slip out in a breathy whisper, and I know I should probably be embarrassed that I'm gawking, but I'm not. I've never seen anything like them before. I have no clue if I'm awake or asleep, but man, if this isn't reality I seriously need to stop spending all my free time reading werewolf porn and actually converse with a real man.

"I am called Saxon and I only wish to protect you."

"Saxon...right...I'm Leigh," I mumble, still in complete shock. I must be dead or delirious, because at this point it's the only explanation. The boat sways, and Henrietta's metal security cables smash against the hull.

Wait. The only way those would be free was if...

I tear my hands from his, my temples pulsing with each step, and run toward Henrietta's launch pad. Vomit climbs up my throat.

"Where...is...it...?" I manage between short, clipped

breaths. "It should be here. She should be here." Dread settles heavy in my gut, and even though I can't remember what's happened, I know it's bad, and this strange man has something to do with it. "What did you do?"

"Your vessel lies at the bottom of this liquid prison, *Mu Xitall*. You were bleeding and the wet ooze tried to steal your life. I had to tear you from it." His fingers gently trace a tender spot on my forehead, and like a tidal wave, the memory of what happened rushes back to me.

Sneaking onto Henrietta after Elgin fired me. Breaking the record low. The beauty of the bioluminescent life. Then the burning pain radiating through my head after I smashed Henrietta into the cave wall. I'm such an idiot. Of course, I'd manage to hallucinate down there and completely sabotage myself, nearly dying in the process.

"But, how did you find me? I turned off all outgoing communications. Not that I'm not happy to be alive, but I should have died. It doesn't make sense."

He smiles, and even in the dim light, I can see its brilliance. "I awoke to your body's need for healing. Our mate connection is strong."

"Our wh-what?" I sputter. "Wait, what do you mean you *awoke*?"

Swaying with dizziness, I stumble toward my room, and Saxon follows close behind. My head feels like it's about to explode, making it hard to think. I need meds, water, and this damn wetsuit off, then maybe this giant clusterfuck will make sense.

My raw palms sting as I rest them against the counter of my kitchenette. Running through the fragmented memories, I try and organize my thoughts and focus through the pain. "I know I was a dumbass and knocked myself out, but Henrietta's hull wasn't breached. The compartment was intact. Maybe if I can spot her on the sonar, we can retrieve her tomorrow before Elgin shows up and the rest of the team returns..."

"It is no use. The wet ooze consumed the craft as soon as I ripped it open." He covers my hand, and I jerk away, turning to face him for the first time in full light.

"Listen, I already warned you about getting too close—oh, my holy shitnuggets. You're..."

Gray. Ripped. Clawed. Soaking wet and half-naked with full lips and an ass I could bounce a quarter off of.

His lips pull at the corners as my eyes linger on his rock hard abs. There are *ten* of them. "Yours."

"Mine?"

"Yes, *Mu Xitall*. I am yours."

Oh, hell. I do not have the mental capacity for this. One massive life-changing event at a time.

"Okay, but what *are* you?"

"I am a Revari male. One of the strongest. I have traveled galaxies to find you, and I desire nothing more than to touch—"

He reaches out, but I flinch and he withdraws.

Damn it. Come back! I think?

I don't know what's crazier. That the *creature* who just saved my life is trying to caress my face, or that I want to let him. Nearly dying is really messing with my head.

Is this what shock is like?

"And you found me at the bottom of the ocean." I draw out the words, hoping if I say them slower they'll make sense, but they don't. It's still freaking insane and impossible and yet here we are.

"We found each other. If not for you, it is possible I would have remained buried in my travel pod forever."

Oh, perfect. Because, why not?

In a single day, I've managed to make history, nearly get myself killed, and lose all proof of my accomplishments and life's work. Oh, and there's the whole sinking a twenty-million dollar craft and getting fired, so why not add waking up a mysterious man-creature who's been sleeping under the ocean for God knows how long?

I take in his face once again, still engrossed by how insanely unique his features are.

A broad nose with little slits on either side of his nostrils, brilliant gold eyes, high cheekbones and lips so thick I can practically taste them.

Wait, where did that come from? And why do I all of a sudden *want* to be near him? Something about him feels, I don't know, familiar? And now that I can really see him, I can't *stop* seeing him. My eyes won't cooperate and look away. He's just so wonderfully...*alien*.

Get a grip, Leigh. Normal people don't act like this. You just ruined your life. Focus on that, then on the hot mystery guy standing over you.

Before, outside in the dark, I was less stabby than I should have been. Granted I do have a head wound, but still. Even on the island, I never walk alone by myself at night, never open my door, but waking up to him confused and disoriented? It took me a whole thirty seconds to believe his outrageous story. Why was that? Why do I feel like I can trust him and we only just met?

Because you're lonely, horny, and out of a job.

Suddenly realizing I've been having this entire inner monologue while blatantly staring at him, I look away and try like hell not to blush. I lift my eyes to gauge his response and am met with enough heat to set my boring cotton panties on fire.

Damn it. Stop looking, Leigh! Or, say something, at least.

The satellite phone on the table near my bed rings and

shocks me out of my trance. Worst timing ever. Or maybe, the best? Wait, who would be calling me at this hour?

I try to reach it, but I can't without moving, and Saxon doesn't seem in a hurry to get away from me. "I have to answer this."

Saxon's nostrils flare and the muscle in his jaw ticks. "You are under the control of another? Where is it? I shall liberate you. With me, you will answer to no one."

Wait, did he just grow out his claws?

"No, nothing like that. It's a work phone. It could be my boss. I have to figure out a way to explain why I'm here and why his money is all down there," I say, pointing toward Henrietta's watery tomb.

Rather than moving, Saxon reaches over with one exceptionally sculpted arm, grabs my phone, and hands it to me. Good gracious, he's built like a brick shit house.

"You answer to no one, *Mu—*"

"Shh," I say, pressing a finger to his lips. Saxon cocks a brow but holds his tongue. By the time I pick it up, whoever tried to call has given up. A minute or so later, a beep signals a new voicemail. Actually, there are six of them.

What the heck?

Still unable to keep my eyes off him, I press play on the most recent and watch Saxon as he stares down at my hand, then swallow a gasp. Smooth and wet, his tongue slips out between his parted lips and *wraps* around my finger—tasting it. Warmth cascades down my body in waves, and my mouth goes dry. How am I supposed to concentrate? And more importantly, why the hell haven't I pulled my hand away?

"Hello, Dr. Lennox. This is Walter Hardeman, head of accounting for Daxx Corp. I'm sorry to bother you this late, but after my assistants looked into an anonymous tip we received early this morning, I was notified of several inconsistencies from

your Nautilus Five project. Please contact me immediately so we can correct the issue."

Well, if that isn't a big helping of karma, I don't know what is. My funding has disappeared over the past several months, and I know it's Elgin's doing. It has to be. No one else is allowed to sign off on expenditures. There's an entire committee that's supposed to pass the budget and approve things, but I have a sneaking suspicion Elgin hasn't even brought half the things I've asked for to them. And if he has, he hasn't given me the funds they allotted.

Daxx Corp just let Elgin fire me in not so many words, stole my chance at making history, and now they want my help? Ha. Screw that. I hope they investigate and catch him red-handed. Especially considering I have copies of all my requests he denied and screenshots of our conversations.

Elgin can go screw himself. Daxx Corp, too.

The most wonderful warmth blooms in my chest as Saxon wraps his arms around me and tucks me under his chin. I tense, already alight with adrenaline and ready to push him away, but can't muster the energy to refuse his magnetic touch.

This is ridiculous. He's a stranger—an *alien,* no less. He shouldn't feel this good, but as the heartbeat thumping in his neck syncs with mine, the anxiety jackhammering my insides eases, and for the first time since he pulled me from the sea, I feel like I can breathe.

Words dance on the tip of my tongue as I try to fill the awkward silence, but my mind's so overloaded I can't even begin to find something coherent to say. "I should..."

Get away from here. Pack my shit and run. Find a giant flat rock somewhere to hide under and die...

I've spent my whole life trying to prove I'm not the same piece of crap alcoholic my father is. He squandered his genius and other people's investment money and ruined himself and our family in the process.

It took me years of hard work for anyone to take me seriously. Hell, even my mother begged me to enter beauty pageants and talent shows rather than sit in my room and study science journals. But I'm just not that girl. I never will be.

This is the only thing I've ever wanted and still, I managed to screw it up. Again. It's starting to look like I can't outrun our family curse, after all.

My lip trembles, and I fight to reel in my tears. They won't solve anything. Henrietta won't magically appear because I stand here bawling like a big fat baby, but I've reached my max out of pocket for shitty life events. It's either this or explode into a billion pieces.

Saxon curls around me, strengthening our embrace. "There is no need for explanation, *Mu Xitall*. Our souls speak without words. Be still, allow them to soothe each other."

Yeah, but can we talk about what you just did with your tongue?

The longer we stand here wrapped around each other, the drowsier I get. The tiny chime on my clock dings and just like a back-up alarm, Binky starts to wail for her snack. I swear this cat eats more than I do.

Saxon tenses and shoves me behind him. "This tiny beast dares to demand your attention? I can dispose of it if you wish."

Hard rock-like ridges rise across his shoulders, and black cascades across his gray skin.

What is that? Some kind of armor? He can't seriously be trying to fight my cat.

"Oh, no, you don't!" I yell, ducking under his arm and throwing myself between them. "You put those angry looking shoulder pads away right now and simmer down."

Saxon stops, still glaring at my overweight foot warmer, and lets out an eerily similar growl. "I do not care for her tone or the way in which she demands to be served. It is unacceptable."

My mouth drops open in shock when he makes the sound again and Binky runs underneath my bed. She hates it under there because she's so overweight it's impossible for her to get out alone. "Did you just *talk* to my cat?"

"I warned her this type of insolence will not be tolerated in my presence and that she would be punished accordingly if she chooses to disobey my command."

I snort, amused at the idea of my grumpy fur ball getting told off in her own language. She's been strutting around like a little dictator since I rescued her from the beach as a kitten.

"How did you...? Wait, did she say anything back?"

Saxon's narrow brow furls. "The words are too filthy to repeat, *Mu Xitall*. I have never heard a creature that speaks with such contempt."

This must be his first encounter with a cat.

"For some reason, that doesn't surprise me. Some people think her kind are tiny little overloads who came to Earth to mess with us for their own amusement," I say, yanking up the bed enough for her to get out and then shuffling back to the kitchen to toss some food in her bowl.

"Is that the name of this planet? Earth?"

"Yes, it is—whoa..." The room spins, and dark spots cloud my vision when I try to fill her water bowl.

Saxon takes it from my hands and guides me to the edge of my bed. "You need to rest. I will ensure the tiny overlord survives."

"No offense. I know you saved my life, but I don't know you, and sleeping with a strange guy on board probably isn't the best idea."

He tilts his head, almost as if he's trying to make sure he understands. "You fear me, still?"

"I don't fear you. That's the problem. I *should,* but it feels like I've known you forever. I'm not sure how it works on your planet, but here? I don't allow strange men to watch me sleep."

Saxon stiffens as something akin to rage flashes in his golden eyes. "They have tried? These *men* you speak of?"

I wait for him to crack a smile, but he doesn't. He's seriously pissed at the idea of some guy just being near me, and damn. I kind of like it.

"Relax, I haven't had a man in my place since...well, ever really. I work too much."

The throbbing behind my temples eases slightly when my head hits the pillow, and Binky's collar jingles as she finds her place at the corner of my bed. Giving in to the demand of my heavy lids for just a second, I close my eyes. I'm not going to sleep. Just rest a little until I can think straight.

A heavy weight settles beside me, and a hand wraps around mine. Warmth spreads over my skin, cementing me in place, and Binky starts to purr. "You should not fear me, *Mu Xitall.* It is our connection that allows you to feel my intentions. Sleep. Our connection will ease our fatigue."

I crack an eye open, using the last of my waning energy to make sure I don't need to get between Binky and Saxon. *What?* The little harlot's curled up against Saxon, massaging his arm like he didn't just threaten to send her to kitty heaven. I cock a brow, and Saxon smirks. "She has accepted me as her alpha and seeks my favor."

Binky hates men and always has. In the five years I've had her, she's never once allowed one to pet her, but with Saxon, she's belly up, begging for attention.

I can't blame her. He might look like a hot, scary alien mash-up but if I were a cat, I'd be against those abs in a heartbeat. Even now with him this close, abandoning all logic and crawling over Binky to steal her spot is sounding more and more appealing.

Well, once Elgin realizes what happened tonight, my professional and social life are going to end, so...

Saxon pulls me closer, moving Binky out of the way, and I don't protest. I don't have the chance because as soon as I'm flush against his naked chest, my consciousness fades, and I'm lulled to sleep by the feel of his breath on my cheek.

CHAPTER FOUR

Leigh

I jerk awake to the sound of footsteps. Binky, you little—*wait.* Those are way too loud to be the cat. My room is tiny and with only a thin wall separating me from the rest of my on-board quarters, I can hear everything. There shouldn't be anyone else in here.

Heart in my throat, I grab the metal wrench I keep beside my bed for emergencies. My head spins, and I stumble—half-asleep— toward the thin wooden door that separates me from my kitchenette. Did I drink last night? My thoughts are fuzzy, yesterday's events a jumbled haze.

The sun peeks through my window slats, and Binky's curled up on her corner of the bed. Useless little brat. There's a stranger lurking steps away and she didn't even wake up. I swear, after she kicks the bucket, I'm getting a dog.

Ugh. No, I won't. I'll be devastated and probably get a cat just like her, but still...

A loud thud followed by a clap of thunder vibrates my door. It's one of the crappiest parts of having the closest room to the deck.

The footsteps quicken. Shit, okay. Come on, Leigh, what was it you learned in self-defense class? Balls, throat, and nose. Or was it balls, face, and foot? I can't remember what you're supposed to hit to bring your opponent down. I'll just aim for whatever's closest.

Worse comes to worst, a good punch to the dick ought to do it. It's never failed me before.

Sucking in a deep breath, I tiptoe out of my bedroom, tightening my grip on the wrench. Binky howls her usual good morning, and I turn back to where she's still sprawled out, trying to shut her up before whoever's out there realizes we're awake.

"What are you doing, *Mu Xitall?*"

The sound of his voice sizzles across my consciousness. *Saxon.*

It's raspy, and I swear I can feel it all the way to my toes. The tips of my fingers brush against muscular thighs and the slick smoothness of the pants stretched across them. Coming all at once, memories of yesterday's disaster rush back to me. Losing Henrietta. Getting shafted by Elgin. Nearly losing my life, and Saxon saving me from the depths of the ocean.

I sneak a quick side glance, hoping he doesn't notice. Yep. There's *definitely* a hot alien behind me.

Heat radiates off him, seeping into the muscles of my back as he stands close behind me. "I was just, eh...I thought you were a random stranger who boarded the ship without permission."

He chuckles, then swipes the hair off the back of my shoulders, sending goosebumps coving my skin. "No being would make it past the wet ooze surrounding us without me knowing. I have spoken at length with the creatures that dwell beneath the surface. They too, watch for danger."

"Oh, yeah? First my cat, and now the fish?" I ask, cracking a smile. Surely, he's joking, right? People just don't talk to whales.

Butterflies tumble around in my belly when I turn and catch sight of his handsome face. The few rays of sun that peek through the thunder clouds rolling overhead are nothing compared to the brilliance of his eyes. With flecks of gold, they shine like yellow sapphires when the light hits them just right.

Step away from the hot alien, Leigh.

His lips turn up once my gaze connects with his, He takes my hand and presses my fingertips to a small opening at the base of his throat. "Here. All my kind are born with the distinct ability to master sound. With the assistance of the implant in our brains, we are able to analyze and repeat any spoken language. This includes those that do not use words."

"Fascinating... You said your kind. You mean the Revari? Isn't that what you called yourself?"

"Such an inquisitive beautiful creature..." Saxon says to himself. "Yes, I am of planet Revaris. What do you call yourselves? The Earthen?"

"Oh, no. Nothing near as cool as that. We're called humans."

The tiny hole at the base of his throat opens and closes when he swallows. Now that I know what it can do, I can't stop staring at it. There are so many possibilities and wonderful things to learn from the creatures around us, and to have someone who can talk to them?

"That's insane," I whisper. The words slide out before I can contain them and Saxon furrows his brow. "Oh, no! I don't mean that in a literal way." I rush to explain. "It's just that

Earth has never seen beings from other planets. No one here knows they—you—exist."

"Your kind do not explore the stars?" Saxon asks with a faraway tone. The tip of his claw gently traces my features one by one.

"They do, they just haven't found any other life yet."

"So, I am the first." There's an awkward silence and a hint of concern in his eyes that sits wrong. A strange wave of protectiveness hits me right in the chest, and it has me desperate for something to make his worry go away.

"You said you could process any sounds, right?" I ask, running over to the old digital sound player on my dresser. The buttons stick, but after mashing them unnecessarily hard, Clair De Lune starts streaming through the tiny speaker.

The music weaves its way through the cabin, warming the space, and I hum along. Saxon cocks his head and, as the notes play, he stares at me. "You enjoy these sounds," he says, eyes locked on mine. "They stir your soul. I can feel it."

"Yeah, I've always loved classical music," I murmur, still caught up in the melody. By the time I remember he probably wants an explanation, I've left him waiting for nearly a minute. Rather than look annoyed, he's just watching me. "What? Do I look funny or something?"

"No, *Mu Xitall.* I'm merely memorizing your face and how it appears when something pleases you. I wish to give you that face many times over."

I swallow hard, assaulted with flashes of our naked bodies slapping together in my head. There's something about the way he says the word *pleases* that makes my panties feel a little too present. *Oh, hello, ovaries. Nice of you to make yourselves known.*

Saxon's nostrils flare slightly, and he cocks his head once

more like he's studying me. I both like and hate the way he seems to be breaking me down. It makes me feel vulnerable, but at the same time no one's bothered to look so deeply at what makes me tick before. "It is this music that makes you feel this way?" he asks, and red blooms across my cheeks.

No, it's you and those abs, and your beautiful eyes and legs and damn, even your calves are sexy. I've got to calm down and think about something else. Blue cheese. Old, wrinkly balls. Eh, that did it.

"Yep. It's the music." I switch off the song, slightly embarrassed I asked. I'm so off kilter and out of my element, I don't know what to do or how to act. Any sane person would have jumped off the boat and likely died from exhaustion half-way to Saipan trying to get away from him just because of how different he looks, but I didn't.

I don't know if it's because I'm tipping over the edge of crazy, still in shock about Henrietta and my own impending doom, or because whoever or whatever he is, he really is meant for me. I shouldn't even be entertaining the idea but I can't help it.

With clammy hands, I smooth my hair and head toward the kitchen but I don't make it two steps. A perfect replica of Clair De Lune floats through the air, twisting and wrapping itself around me. It's eerie and beautiful and shocking the way he's projecting a melody so close to my heart.

I feel every note in the depths of my soul. Chills spread across my skin, instilling a sense of wonder one only feels when hearing something truly moving for the first time. This symphonic poem has been a staple in my life since I was young, but I've never heard it sound like this. The music carries me closer, and by the time he's finished with the final note, I'm but a breath away.

"That was beautiful," I say, close enough to see the tiny slits on either side of his nose. I hadn't noticed them before. I'm guessing that's part of the anatomy that allowed him to swim me to safety.

Saxon's pupils dilate, and his shoulders curl in slightly as he cups the side of my face and runs his thumb along my jaw.

"I..." The word slips out in a rough whisper. He's staring at me with his sunflower eyes and he smells so good, but before I can finish my thought and say or do something stupid, the weather station starts to blare in Chamorro, then English.

Heavy thunderstorms headed due east. Cloud to ground lightning expected as well as high winds. Take cover.

Wait, if I'm hearing this, then so is the captain of that fancy ass yacht. The rest of the crew is going to come back ahead of schedule. A hollow sense of dread wipes out the few moments of serenity Saxon's voice gave me and gives me a swift kick in the ass.

I can't avoid this any longer. If I was expendable to Elgin before I sank Henrietta, there's no telling what's going to happen now. There are so many news companies planning to live stream the dive. At least four magazines scheduled interviews, and the entire scientific community is waiting for Henrietta to make history.

Elgin's going to go apeshit when he finds out, and I can't be here when he does.

Binky jumps up on the windowsill and starts pawing at the blinds—something she only does when the storms coming in are particularly rough.

"We need to come—go, I mean go." I cringe and clear my throat. "We need to get back to the shore before the storm hits and everyone finds out what's happened."

Saxon tilts his head, gaze locked on my red cheeks. "I can

smell your fear. If this vessel cannot sustain us, I can. My body is hard enough to protect you, no matter the circumstance."

Hard? Why, yes. Yes, it is.

"That's not it. I'm not worried about the storm. I'm worried about people seeing you. And my boss figuring out I ruined the launch. I screwed up, Saxon. Really bad. And I don't want to be here when everyone else finds out."

Saxon straightens to his full height, giving my face one last caress before dropping his hand. His eyes narrow as Binky hops down from the window and starts dancing around his legs—wrapping her saucy little tail around his ankles. I don't know what she's saying to him, but he doesn't seem amused.

"Then we will leave. I will protect you no matter the circumstance."

"I actually have zero doubts you can, but if it's okay with you, I'd like to avoid any conflict and just head back now to be safe."

"I am with you, *Mu Xitall*. Anywhere and always."

Before I drag Saxon outside to the little dinghy stored on the port side of the boat, I grab the radio and try to reach Anya. She gets a little crazy when the weather's bad. Okay, so she's always a paranoid, conspiracy theory-believing hot mess, but it's worse when a storm blows through. Probably because she's convinced the government controls the weather.

I have to give her a heads up. She'll flip her lid if she hears it from the news first and assume I'm dead or that Elgin's made me disappear. She's always been worried that he'd steal my designs and take all the credit, and now I'm wondering if maybe, she was right.

She doesn't have a phone and refuses to keep anything around her with a GPS signal. She'll only talk to me on our secret radio channel, and I need to reassure her I'm safe. If not, she'll come looking for me, and lord knows that's the last thing we need now that Saxon's barged into my life.

Since I first stumbled across her on the beach and chopped the head off a snake lurking behind her, she's been my shadow —taking me under her wing to "protect." Scanning my apartment for bugs, altering my radio to keep our channel safe, insisting I don't go certain places at night.

She's always mumbling about how the government's out to get her. Hell, I don't even think Anya's her real name. It's a risk to take the time to call her, but she's important to me.

"Green Goose, this is Henrietta six-nine. Do you copy?"

Saxon's brow furrows at the incoming static and likely, the ridiculous call signs we've assigned ourselves. I fought with her for weeks, but she insisted I come up with a pseudonym, and I eventually gave in.

My sub's government name might have been the Nautilus Five, but the moment the idea came out of my mouth, Henrietta was born. A tear wells in the corner of my eye, and I swipe it away before it can fall.

You can be sad later, but right now you've got to find a way to get yourself out of this mess. Talk to Anya. Make sure she's cool, then figure out what to do about Elgin and Saxon.

"Copy that, Henrietta six-nine, I'm here. The birds are flying and the sun has yet to set."

My lips still as I try to remember the meaning behind the code.

Ugh, I don't have time for this.

Birds are drones, and what does the sun mean again? One of these days, I'm going to find a normal friend...

Oh, who am I kidding? No, I won't.

"Good, good. Are the kids listening?" I ask, knowing that she won't talk for long if she thinks whatever flew over her house earlier has tapped into her communication system.

"They're taking a nap. What color is the sun?" *No one's listening. Are you safe and alone?*

"Blue," I say, unable to hide the edge of exhaustion in my voice. It takes so much effort to talk to her. Sometimes, a little too much. "It's blue, like always. Listen, Green Goose, I'm tired. I took Henrietta out last night and something went really wrong. I can't say much now. But I'll fill you in later. I'm about to head back home. Make sure you get inside. The weather's supposed to be—"

The boat whines as a heavy gust of wind presses down on us from the east. Caught off guard by the sudden sway, my finger slips off the radio, and I'm thrown to the side. But instead of smashing into the wall, I'm flush against the hard ridges of Saxon's abs.

"Henrietta six-nine, are you there?" The sound of Anya's voice blares through the static in the line, but I can barely hear it over the thump of my heartbeat in my ears.

Warmth pools in my belly, then spreads out like wildfire across my skin. I'm trembling—not from the air conditioner on the boat, but from the intensity of whatever's passing between us. Like icy air sweeping through a heated room, it steals my breath and has me floundering.

"Leigh? Talk to me. What's happening?" Anya calls out, but I can't answer. Saxon is all I can see and smell and hear.

With one hand, Saxon steadies a glass on my desk and holds me with the other. Unable to resist, I lean in, pressing myself closer against him. He's just so warm, so safe, so...*everything.*

What is happening to me?

The horizontal slits in his eyes widen, and his jaw strains. "*Mu Xitall...*"

"Saxon," I manage. The radio hits the floor with a thud and, before I can blink, my back is up against the wall and both his hands are in my hair. His lips hover just above mine, but he doesn't kiss me.

With nostrils flared, he licks his lips. "You smell of the most delicious fruit. I only desire to taste you. I have waited so long..." he mumbles, pressing his lips to the side of my neck. A burst of tingles blooms with every light touch, and as he kisses his way down to my collarbone, the sensations combine and slide right between my thighs.

He feels *so good* and all logic goes right out the window.

Like a marionette, I fall limp in his arms, savoring every second of the way his lips dance across my skin until a loud crack of lightning sends Binky barreling into my legs.

Nothing says get *a hold of yourself, bitch* like a set of kitty claws gouging your skin.

"Okay, time out," I say, trying to gain my composure. "I need a second to think." I try to gauge his reaction, but my insatiable need for him flares, and my brain shuts down. I'm wet as hell and more turned on than I've ever been, and I have no clue what I'm doing. "Gah, you're so hot. Why are you so hot?"

Shit, did I say that out loud?

Saxon groans and tightens his grip on my hair, letting his teeth score the shell of my ear. The way he pulls at the strands burns in the most delicious way, and a tiny yelp escapes before I can reel it in. Rather than attack my lips like I really want him to, his rough hold turns soft and he tips up my face.

"Forgive me. Your scent...it calls to me, disarms my restraint."

Saxon's chest is heaving—the taut lines of his abdomen flexing with every deep breath, and it *hurts* to peel myself off of him and back away.

"You're not the only one, but right now we've got to get the hell out of here. Once we're safe..." *I'm going to lick every single inch of your body.* "We'll spend some time and figure *us* out."

He nods, jaw clenched tight like it's taking everything he has not to pounce on me, and grabs the thickness of his cock through his pants. Oh, sweet mercy, it fills his hands and they're twice the size of mine. Another loud thunderclap shakes the windows, and I flinch.

"Your planet fucking sucks," he grunts, readjusting his length once more, then stomps through the door into the rain.

CHAPTER FIVE

Leigh

Getting Saxon into the dinghy was easier than I thought it would be. I wish I could say the same for Bink. She hates it and has been clinging to my alien since we sped off. I've royally screwed this up, and the closer we get to shore, the more reality starts to punch me in the face.

At first, I had hope that a tropical storm would magically manifest and I'd have more time to figure out what to do about Elgin, but the rain is set to pass by the end of the day and the crew would rat on me anyway. As much as I love them, they aren't my friends. Not really. Elgin hired them, and they report directly to him.

I have no doubt he's going to shame me and publicly tear me to shreds. There will be articles comparing me to my father and a whole gossip train floating through the scientific community blacklisting me from any other jobs. Henrietta is my baby. I built her from the ground up, and my research—my designs—

are just that. Mine. Whether Elgin fires me are not, he doesn't deserve to take the credit for himself.

If I could just call Sterling and explain it to him myself, I could tell him about all the shady stuff Elgin's done with his money and maybe, he'd let me keep my job...

I shake my head, trying to banish the insane plan forming before I do something dumb and peek out at Saxon as he scans the horizon for threats.

When he's near, I can't think clearly. It's like there's an off switch in my brain and all the blood goes to my lady bits. What am I supposed to do with him? And for that matter, what do I *want* to do?

Well, what I'd really, *really*, like to do is get us all hot and heavy, but that doesn't exactly solve our problems right now. Especially not this close to land.

Lighting strikes the water near the stern, and I increase our speed. I live less than two miles from shore, and we're so close. If I can just beach this thing on the sand, we can make it to my place relatively unnoticed.

The boat starts rocking harder, and Saxon tightens his grip on my hand. "*Mu Xitall*, the wet ooze stirs beneath us, and the sky is discharging electrical ions at a higher pace."

"Yeah, I know. We're almost back. I'll hop out as soon as we get close and help get us ashore."

"I will guide us."

"No, Saxon. Really, that's not—" Before I can finish, he's hopped over the side of the dinghy and into the water. "Saxon! Damn it, wait. You could get hurt!"

Or send us onto the rocks, or tip us over...

Panic tightens my chest as waves pelt against the side of the boat and rain stings my eyes. Why would he jump out so far away from shore? And how is he breathing underwater like that?

The moment the bow touches sand, I jump over the side, trudging through the water to yell at him.

"What were you thinking jumping into the water like that? Are you insane?"

Ignoring my question, he lifts me up. "The wet ooze threatened you once, *Mu Xitall*. It does not deserve the honor of caressing your skin."

Oh, sweet mercy. This is some romance novel shit. Clutched in his granite arms, he carries me a few feet, sets me down on dry sand, and goes back for Binky who's only too happy to curl against him. Never mind he's soaking wet and she hates water, the little tart's purring like she's in heat.

Saxon hands her to me, then wraps me up in his arms. "You are chilled, and I can feel your exhaustion. I will carry you, *Mu Xitall*. Show me where you call home."

You. You're home. The words are on the tip of my tongue but I swallow them knowing how crazy they'd sound.

Even with blurry eyes, I don't miss the look of reverence on his face when he stares at me, inspecting me for any subtle need. How is it a being I just met can look at me like this and make me feel it all the way in my bones? He makes me want to feel that way for him, and in some ways, I already do.

Warmth slides down my spine, hitting me right between the thighs and I swear if he keeps looking at me like this, I'm going to launch myself at him.

I have no clue what I'm going to do about Elgin and my job. The only thing I know is that I can't leave Saxon. Whatever I do, wherever I go, he's coming with me.

I mean how hard can it be to hide a big gray alien?

It might sound crazy, but something inside me stirred awake the second I saw Saxon's eyes and it's been yelling at me ever since. Sometimes when the universe speaks, you need to shut the hell up and listen. Even if she sounds like a raving lunatic.

"Leigh? Is that you?" I hear yelled from the other side of the sand. *Shit.* Despite the wind and the noise from the crashing waves, I recognize the voice instantly. Joseph, one of the local public safety officers tasked with guarding the island against drug traffickers and illegal smuggling. He's never this far down the beach. Of course, he'd decide to actually do his job the one day my life nearly comes to an end.

A deep growl vibrates Saxon's chest, and he stiffens. "A male approaches and he is armed."

"I know. Hurry. Put this on."

Binky protests when I wiggle out of Saxon's arms but shuts right the hell up when I toss her to him. Any other time, I'd be cracking up at the way he catches her like she has some kind of infectious disease, but right now we don't have time for humor. Joseph is almost close enough to see how very different my alien is.

My alien, huh?

I shove my raincoat at him. "Cover yourself. I have to make this guy go away before he sees you. Stay here and don't move."

"If he touches you, I am not sure I can control myself."

His hand feels impossibly warm when I give it a squeeze, trying to give him some quick reassurance. "He won't. I'll be right back."

Mud and sand stick to my soles, making my short journey toward Joseph take twice as long. You'd think after spending nearly a decade here I'd be used to the feel of wet sand but it still makes me cringe every time.

Blinking through the rain, I do my best to smile and seem remotely normal. "Hey, what in the hell are you doing all the way out here in this shit weather? Shouldn't you be at Kiko's sucking it up at darts?"

Kiko's is a local bar and the only place I've actually seen Joseph. I knew he patrolled the shore because he never shuts up about it, but I haven't ever seen him in action. He spent the first six months I was here bugging me from across the room and jabbering non-stop until I eventually let him sit with me. It was a huge mistake.

He's like a lost puppy who's desperate for attention.

Now, if I want to grab a drink and have some peace and quiet I have to go in right after lunch. Not that I've been able to for the last six months since I was pushing hard to get ready for Henrietta's launch.

Damn, I really miss my girl.

"Me?" he asks. "What about—damn it, hold on..." The hood of Joseph's raincoat flaps back and forth so hard it's sticking to his eyes and covering up half his face. Watching him fight with it so he can respond is actually pretty amusing. "Fucking cheap uniforms. What are you doing out here, Leigh? You getting something last minute for the launch?"

Ugh, does everyone know about the dive? Of course, they do. This island is tiny and half of it is basically overgrown forest.

"Sure am. Left some stuff at my place that I need. You picked a fantastic day to start giving a shit about your job."

"I'm only down here because Tomas spotted your dinghy getting hammered with some pretty strong swells. You should really check the radar before being that far from shore in one of those little things. You could have gotten yourself killed."

"Ah, thanks. Appreciate you looking out for me. Now piss off. It's gross out here. I'm going home."

He chuckles and looks over my shoulder. I can't explain how but I know Saxon is glaring at him and two seconds away from charging over and flinging him into the ocean.

"Nice raincoat. You should tell your man to size up." He

squints, trying to focus, and lets out a slow whistle. "And to get a tan. Damn. He's pale as hell. Where'd you find him? The bottom of the sea?"

Heh. Not fucking funny, Joseph.

Saxon's only partially covered by my second-hand sunflower raincoat. The hood obscures his face, and he's wearing the tight black pants, but his feet and both forearms are sticking out.

Not to mention his broad chest and super defined abs. The coat is too small to close in the front.

Joseph can see him well enough to notice his skin, but with how hard the rain is pelting us, there's no way he can see much else. I just need to get this conversation over with and get Saxon back to my place.

A quick glance at Joseph's uniform tells me he's not wearing the body cams they normally do when patrolling, so, thank God for that. This soggy weather is actually useful for once.

"You might want to keep your voice down. He's pretty sensitive about his fashion."

"Hey, as long as he takes care of you, Leigh, he can walk around in a fuckin' tutu for all I care. Just make sure your dinghy's gone before the weekend's over. I'm here until Sunday night and can make sure no one messes with you, but you'll get ticketed if anyone else catches you leaving it on the beach."

I give him a faux salute. "Sir, yes, sir."

"Get the fuck out of here with that. I'll see you later." He turns and jogs back to where he parked his car, and the anxiety that's wrapped its way around my lungs doesn't uncoil until his butt's in the seat.

I can't get back to Saxon and Binky fast enough. I'm tired, and my head still aches from smacking it against Henrietta's hull.

"He's gone. Come on, let's go." I start to head toward the road but let out a squeal when Saxon lifts me up without warning. Binky hops off his shoulder and reluctantly settles on my chest. I swear the little tart would abandon me for him.

"Whoa, I can walk. You don't have to carry me."

Saxon tightens his grip and grunts, and I swear, I can feel it all the way down to my toes. "It is either carry you or track down the male you just spoke with and maim him for being near you. I am a logical being, *Mu Xitall*. But my attraction to you goes beyond rational thought."

"All right, then. You don't have to tell me twice."

CHAPTER SIX

Saxon

Her golden hair sits like a crown upon her head as she seeks refuge in my arms, and it takes all that is within me not to beg her to quench my thirst for her. The softness of her curves are hidden beneath layers of fabric, but just the hint of their warmth...

By the ancients, if I'd known the fires her scent alone would stoke, I'd have cut out my own tongue for my foolish resistance to leave Revaris in the first place. I did not understand.

When the elders first told me I was one of the Exune—the chosen group of Revari males meant to find their mates on other worlds—I was angry. As males, we are taught from a young age the immense importance of taking a female and curating the mate bond. I spent years aching for the one meant for me, then to be told I must wait longer?

I was pissed.

When we left Revaris and headed into the great black hole, I had little hope to find her.

But then her need stirred me awake—the familiarity of her energy slamming into me like an armor-wrapped fist—and I knew it was the ancient sky spirits themselves who had placed her within reach. She is mine, created for me in every way, and I will not forget what has been gifted me.

Liquid falls from the sky, pelting my female, and no matter how I hold her, she cannot escape. This damned planet is so wet. My cock throbs with each step, and after tasting my Leigh, even for the briefest of seconds, I am struggling to tame my desire for her.

Her cheek shifts against my skin as she tries to cover the tiny beast in her arms and protect it from the liquid pouring down. I do not understand the benefit of such a creature. It offers nothing but the softness of its pelt, yet demands every-thing. Its fangs are far too small to take down predators, and judging by the density of its build, it is not made for combat. So, what does it do?

My female leans up, cupping her hand around her eyes to shield them from the violent wind. "We're here. Just put me down and I'll grab my keys."

A growl builds in my throat, and I want to protest but I silence the selfish desire. I do not ever wish to let her go, but until she truly understands the extent of our connection, her body is not mine to command. The honor of plunging into her sweet flesh must be given, but when I finally seat myself between her thighs and feel her shudder beneath me, she will know...

Our existence begins and ends with one another, and I will protect her at all costs.

Cool air wraps around my skin as she slides from my arms, taunting me, but when she grabs my hand to pull me inside, my need for her hardens against my suit.

She closes her dwelling, a place made of some sort of metal

and painted wood. No sign of programmable weapons or moni-
toring devices. This is where she has been living? Unsecured
and free for any male who wishes to force his way through the
door? How has such a beautiful creature survived alone?

The tiny overlord jumps from her arms and disappears, and
for the first time since we met, I have my female all to myself.

Her feet drag in exhaustion as she trudges over to a cush-
ioned seat of some sort and collapses onto it. She still wears the
thin covering she threw on right before she fell asleep and her
skin is far too pale. I despise being so ill prepared to care for
her. If this were Revaris, I would have placed her in a natural
spring and massaged away her fatigue hours ago, but here?

She needs warmth and nutrition and I do not even know
what food her kind eat. With only the lower half of my suit, I
have little to offer her in the way of clothing, but if I could just
find...

My female's eyes grow heavy as she fights to stay awake, so
I do not rouse her. Using her scent as a guide, I find my way to
her sleeping quarters, grab the first warm covering I see, and lay
it beside her. She stirs and answers my efforts with a smile.
"You got me fresh clothes? Sorry I'm being so lame. I feel like I
haven't slept in days."

"You are tired, *Mu Xitall*. Change and rest. I will guard
your dwelling."

Her tired smile twists into a gasp. "Oh, shit, I'm a terrible
host! My mother's probably rolling over in her grave! You have
to be starving." She jerks up and scurries off toward a small
room in the corner with a large cold box. "I don't have much,
but I'm sure there's something in here..."

Several clanging sounds ring out, and she struggles to open
a jar. Without thought, I take it from her hands and pry the lid
free. Her eyes linger on my forearms, and I lean in, unable to
control my need to be close to her.

Her pupils dilate, and a rush of pride swells in my chest. She feels it, too. Our connection is growing. The longer I am near her and ignore my instinct to mate, the harder it is to respect her desire for distance.

My female clears her throat and drops her gaze to the flat, white sponge she is preparing. "Keep it in your pants, Leigh," she mutters under her breath while she spreads brown and purple goo on the two pieces of fluff then slaps them together. "All right, dinner is served."

"What is the name of this?" I ask, putting the bland concoction to my lips. I will eat what my female made for me, no matter the taste.

"Peanut butter and jelly. It's not exactly gourmet, but it's all I've got."

The fluff goes down like a thick paste, but surprisingly enough, does not taste as terrible as it looks. " It is del-i-ci-ous, *Mu Xitall*," I force out with my tongue stuck to the roof of my mouth.

She snorts and hands me a glass of wet ooze. "Here, you'll need this." I cock a brow, already irritated by its attempts to take her from me earlier. "It's just water, Saxon. Drink it."

"It tried to steal you," I growl.

"Right, juice it is then." She pours me a glass of something sweet, then leans heavily on the counter. Cradling her in my arms feels like second nature, and when she relaxes in my hold, the edge of my wild desire for her eases.

"You have fed me. Your mother will no longer roll. Sleep now."

She says nothing for a moment, only studies me. "I don't think I can. To be honest, this whole day has been so insane, I'm afraid if I do, I'll wake up, you'll be gone, and I'll still be inside Henrietta at the bottom of the ocean."

I guide her to the room that holds her scent the strongest.

"Then I will rest alongside you and carry you through your dreams."

Leigh

My phone vibrates on my bedside table and nearly falls to the floor. Thank goodness it's on silent because an exhausted Saxon still snores softly beside me. His arm's draped across my belly and his face is tucked in close to mine.

I thought he was beautiful awake, but asleep he's damn near breathtaking. No wonder I can't seem to keep myself in check around him. I don't know anyone with a pulse who could.

Making sure to pull the covers over my head to muffle the sound before I listen, I check out who the hell would be calling me this late. Or is it early? With black out curtains and a partially healed head wound, it's hard to tell what time it is.

The clock on screen informs me it's only mid-afternoon. Well, that makes sense. I guess I haven't been sleeping for as long as I thought.

A number I don't recognize pops up on screen, calling a second time, and a notification for sixteen voicemails streams across the bottom. I shouldn't to listen to them. I already know they're going to make me feel like crap, but my anxiety and OCD won't let me refuse.

There's no telling what kind of shit show is going on at the boat. The rest of the crew has to be back by now and there's no way they haven't noticed Henrietta's gone. Or that I'm gone. And when they go to check the footage they won't find it either since I turned off the upload before I went down.

I've made such a mess of this.

The first six are just panicked messages from my team trying to figure out where I am and where Henrietta is, but the next has me stopping dead in my tracks.

Risa's panic-filled voice pours through the speaker. "Leigh, where is the Nautil—Henrietta? And where are you? I don't know what's happening or what's going on but you need to call me. People are saying things. Things that I know can't possibly be true but it's gone beyond the team and law enforcement is involved. Please, wherever you are. Call me. This is bad."

Wait, what is she talking about? They're calling the cops on me for sinking Henrietta? I don't understand. With shaking hands, I scroll through to the next voice message and listen to all of them.

No. This isn't possible.

Message after message plays and each one says a variation of the same thing. Not only are people wondering where I am and what happened to Henrietta, but apparently, they're calling to tell me I'm under investigation for stealing and mishandling funds. And an officer boarded the boat today with cuffs. Which means they could show up here at any moment. Thank goodness they have a tiny police force or I'd already be in jail.

Someone's trying to frame me, and really, there's only one person it could be.

Elgin? But why?

Sliding out of bed quietly is nearly impossible with the way Binky and Saxon sleep, but I manage and tiptoe into the bathroom to throw some water on my face. This can't be real life. I mean, what would have happened if I had stayed? If Elgin had never fired me and stolen my dive. What? Would they have carted me away in cuffs when I came up for my victory party?

How long has Elgin been framing me for these crimes? And more importantly, how am I just now finding out about it?

I feel like such an idiot. I knew I should have said something the moment I noticed Elgin cutting corners and denying my requests but I assumed as long as his crazy was focused the other way it wouldn't bite me in the ass. I'd just keep my head down, do my work, make history, and then branch out after I'd made a name for myself.

Yet, here I am—ass thoroughly chewed into little bits, trying to figure out how to keep myself out of jail. And how to keep Saxon hidden.

How am I going to get myself out of this?

My computer at the lab! I keep all my important stuff on several external hard drives—one of which is with Anya—but my laptop has all the proof I need to show Elgin's the one misappropriating the funding. I don't even have access to the project accounts.

Rather than risk waking anyone up, I sneak out the front door as quietly as possible, not even bothering to change. There's a slim chance everyone's still on the boat looking for Henrietta and haven't made it back to the lab.

I know I don't have a job, but I can prove I'm innocent and Elgin's the dickhole stealing money, I can keep my freedom at least. The image of Saxon's handsome face lingers as I make my way toward my car.

I can't imagine what me being arrested would mean for him, or what he would do. Something tells me there's no way he'd ever let someone take me away from him, and he'd probably get himself into one hell of a mess trying to keep me safe.

I can't put him in that position. He deserves more than that.

HOLDING MY BREATH, I slide my card through the reader and pray it unlocks. I've done this thousands of times, but this is different. This time I'm breaking into a building that I'm not welcome in to steal a laptop and a whole bunch of confidential communications that, by law, don't belong to me.

Ding. Oh, thank God no one's had the chance to revoke my access yet.

The locks flip open, and I quietly pass through the door, then toss a look behind me to make sure Saxon didn't somehow follow. It feels so dishonest to leave without waking him, but I didn't want to bring him here in case things go sideways. I don't even want to think about what a man like Elgin would do if he knew aliens existed.

The thick leather strap from my cross-body bag bites into my shoulder, but it's the only one I have big enough to fit my work laptop and most of my notebooks.

As always, it's dark, per Elgin's ridiculous rules about leaving the lights on, and it looks completely empty like I hoped. The rest of the crew must still be on the boat. I should have the place to myself.

Since I have a few extra moments, I want to grab my favorite coffee cup. My sister sent it to me for Christmas a few years ago before she decided I was a steaming pile of shit just like our dad and refused to speak to me, and I don't want to leave it behind. It's a custom made picture of me vomiting rainbows and swimming with dolphins. It might seem dumb, but it's the only thing I have of hers to hold on to.

Taking a quick detour to the right, I hurry into the kitchen and search through the cabinets where I always leave it. Wait. Why is it sitting on the counter? I know I washed it and put it up before I left.

The smell of stale coffee and...what is that?—bourbon?—rise from the cup, and my heart skips a beat. We all left for the boat together. No one would have any reason to come in, unless...

"I was wondering when you'd show up."

Nearly jumping out of my skin, I fumble the cup, catching it just before it slams into the ground ,and whirl around to glare at him. "Elgin? What the hell!" I screech. "Why are you just standing there in the dark? Are you trying to give me a heart attack?"

"Of course not. Why on Earth would I want to do that?" He laughs and lifts a flask. "You deserve something far more painful for the shit you just pulled."

Already sensing this conversation is going to go downhill quick, I try to back slip past him but he blocks my way. "I was just going to go pack up my office—"

"Did you enjoy it? Letting me parade around this morning like I was about to make history when you'd sank my most prized possession *in the middle of the fucking ocean!*"

His spittle flies in my face as he screams the last bit, and I flinch at the anger in his voice.

"Look, I can explain," I squeak out, stuck somewhere between trying to bite my tongue and fearing for my life. He's unhinged and drunk. I always thought he was a harmless tool, but his bloodshot eyes are wild and unwieldy.

"No need. I've seen the footage."

The room suddenly gets hot and my throat goes dry. "What are you talking about?" The only footage is inside Henrietta at the bottom of the sea. I made sure to turn everything off but the single inside camera.

"I said, I saw it for myself, you ungrateful brat. You didn't actually think I'd trust you after you sank the Juniper, did you?"

"Elgin, what did you do?" I ask, voice cracking. The last of my bravado drains with the sneer on his face.

"I had Johan insert an undetectable recording device that streamed directly to my private server. I've watched you, Leigh. Every second you've spent inside my machine, pissing away my money..." He takes a long swig, then wipes his mouth on the sleeve of his two hundred dollar shirt. "I will say, those pink shorts of yours quickly became my favorite. They almost made your fumbling around bearable."

Nostrils flaring, I clench my jaw, trying to look intimidating. Elgin might be a guy, but he's barely taller than me and I'm not exactly dainty. "Get out of my way. I'm leaving."

"Like hell you are," he growls, leaning in close enough for me to smell the whiskey on his breath. "I told everyone I was going to make history and I still fucking will. Bring it to me. That *thing* you found down there. I've got way to much riding on this. If you knew the people I owe—"

No. Saxon. No. No. No.

"I'm not sure what you think you saw, but maybe you've had a little too much to drink," I say, fighting to hide the tremble in my voice. "I'll own up to crashing the Nautilus, and you can *try* to blame all the missing money on me, but I'm not going to stand here and let you—"

My body goes numb, adrenaline kicking in and taking over as he reaches out and palms my breast. "You'll do whatever the fuck I say. I own you. Especially after everything I sent to the island police. Bring him to me, or I'll take him myself. You're fucked no matter what, Leigh. How bad is up to you."

Elgin flinches at the sound of glass breaking and the blare of an alarm, and I slam my coffee cup into the side of his face. "You bitch!" he screams, and I take off toward the door.

I can't breathe—can't think. I need to get out. I have to get away and get back to Saxon. I can't let Elgin take him away from me. They'll lock him up and turn him into an experiment. I scream as I turn the corner and run into a hard solid chest. I beat against it, unable to see in the dark, until a familiar pair of arms wraps around me.

"Saxon? How'd you—"

"I am here, *Mu Xitall*. I felt your fear."

"You bitch! You broke my jaw," Elgin screams, and I cringe at the sound.

Saxon roars, shoving me behind him, and starts off toward where Elgin is rolling on the ground, clutching his bloody face. " *Za tra icurasic!*" he growls, then yells something that sounds a whole lot like "*die*."

Oh, shit.

"No, Saxon. You can't!" I yell over the sirens, yanking him back. He stiffens, but lets me pull him back toward the door.

"He *touched* you. His abuse will not go unanswered!" he roars again, and for the first time I notice the green glow surrounding the black armor coating his skin.

"Please, Elgin contracted with the human government to protect this place. They can't find out about you. We have to go," I beg and yank on him again.

His gaze connects with mine, and his wide pupils narrow, no doubt seeing the tears in my eyes. "You will not leave me again," he growls. Anger and fear twist their way through his words and I hate that it's because of me. "I *cannot* lose you. Not when you've only just been found."

"Okay." The weight of that word holds me in place. After this, after what I've just done, after what Elgin has seen, I can't ever leave him again.

Chest heaving, he throws me over his shoulder and takes off at inhuman speed. The rain has yet to relent, but within seconds we're at my car, and anxiety takes hold.

I wiggle out of Saxon's arms, hop in the driver's side and floor it all the way to my house. I run to throw together a bag of mine and Binky's things. Shirts, underwear, my flash drive, an old picture of my sister and niece, and what cash I have on hand. I don't even bother with any of my cards or checks. Elgin will freeze my accounts in a second; there's no point.

My heart sinks.

This is it—my life in just a few items.

Saxon stands unmoving, but I don't look at him. Not yet. Not when there's so much to say, and so little time to do it in.

"*Mu Xitall,* you still tremble. You are safe with me," Saxon whispers, and I nearly crumble under the weight of his hands on my shoulders.

"I know you're angry and I shouldn't have just left like that. We can't stay here, but I know a place. Then...then we'll talk."

After gathering the basics, including my passport and all the records of Elgin I kept, I snag Binky off her bed and finally face my alien. "I'm ready."

CHAPTER SEVEN

Leigh

We run toward the beach—the only place I can think of that might be out of Elgin's reach. One of the local fisherman, Ayuyu, has a hut that he rents under the table to people looking to stay off the grid. It's inside an isolated portion of the island that's long since been overgrown and abandoned. He offered it to me early on when he assumed I was in Saipan running from an abusive ex.

After the great earthquake of 2045 sent a tsunami to wipe out half the island, travel was restricted, both in and out, and citizenship was denied for any outsiders seeking to move here.

Most of the land remaining above sea level was rebuilt, but there's still an entire section that was too decimated to recover.

From what I remember, that's where we're going. Somewhere in the unsafe zone. Hopefully, somewhere Elgin won't think to look for me.

When I slip the cash under the box at his stand, I pray

everything's still where he told me it would be. So many things could go wrong...

It's been years since I've seen him, and Ayuyu's old. He could have died, he could have been arrested, who knows?

A tiny metal box peeks out from the sand near the edge of a cluster of old fishing nets *Please, please...*

"Oh, thank God. They're here." The map is withered but readable, and the keys sit heavy in my hand. "How in the hell are we supposed to get there?" I mutter under my breath. A scooter won't work, and we certainly can't take anything bigger. It won't handle the terrain. No wonder this is a good hiding place, it's virtually impossible to reach.

"You are distressed. Share your concerns, *Mu Xitall*, so that I may relieve you of them."

I rub my eyes and huddle close to the tiny bit of protection the rusted overhang of Ayuyu's stand offers from the rain. "We can't reach it. Not in this weather. It's unsafe, and the journey would take more than a day on foot. I'm just trying to figure out what we can do."

Saxon breaks his silence and wraps his free hand around mine, then brings it to his lips. "As always, I will carry you. I can travel at much higher speeds than your human body allows. Grant me the honor of assisting you."

"After everything I've put you through, you'd do that for me?"

Releasing my hand, he cups my face and gently tips up my chin. "I have searched the universe for you with nothing but the promise of your existence to guide me. My body—my soul— are yours whenever and for whatever purpose you require for as long as my life blood sustains me."

"How are you real?" I blurt out, caught up in emotion. "I feel like I'm going to wake up and all of this will be just a dream."

"I am real, *Mu Xitall*, and in time, I will earn your confidence." He scans the map, then without warning lifts me up and takes off toward the dense forest that hides Ayuyu's refuge.

Saxon

My female stares at the sky above, and though the sharp edges of Earthen plants tear at my feet, shredding the flesh, I do not make a sound. My second-in-command, Warxal had pushed to extend the hardened fibers of our travel suits to encompass our entire form before we set off, and because of this place, I see he was right.

I need to rouse the other males. They too, deserve to live. Deserve the feel of their fated mate in their arms, but with my internal beacon malfunctioning, I cannot not wake them from a distance. I will have to return to the wet ooze and separate from my female—two things I am not sure I can do. I allowed her to leave my side once, and she nearly died.

Her terror lingers. I cannot read her mind, but the imprint of her emotions floats on the surface of her skin and I absorb the sensations and take them on as my own.

She may not register their negative stain on her consciousness, but it is fresh in mine.

Fear. Disgust. Betrayal. Whatever that human did to her has caused her great pain. He will pay for her suffering a thousand-fold.

Honor calls me to destroy him. Cleave the pale skin from his flesh while he screams, but my female demanded I stop and follow, and I did without question.

If I am to prove my worth as her mate and earn passage into the recesses of her soul, I cannot ask for trust if I do not first give it. She will share her thoughts when ready, and for now, I will wait dutifully by her side.

Her heart beats in sync with mine as she clings to the furry overlord she insists on cradling in her arms. Land-dwelling creatures stalk us, matching each of my carefully slowed steps, but none dare to make themselves known. The scents of fear and curiosity swirl in the air. They have seen humans and have grown accustomed to their presence, but they have not encountered a being like me.

As natural predators, they recognize me as the beast I am—the beast that to everyone but my female—I will be. She is mine to protect, and I will not relent when it comes to her safety.

Gleaming in the pale light of the Earthen moon, a small dwelling hides beneath a massive growth of plant life. Nostrils flared, I inhale deeply. No human signatures are present, not for at least another five thousand strides. A deep howl silences the tiny creature noises around me, and the little overlord awakes, stirring in my female's arms.

"Are we there?" she asks, then looks around. "It's so dark, how can you even see?"

"Revari males are made to hunt at night, *Mu Xitall*."

Her heart rate jumps, and she tightens her hold around my neck. "It's so quiet. Why? Is there something out there? Damn, I bet it's big."

"No bigger than me. The beasts here will not be bothering us. Your tiny overlord on the other hand, will not fare so well on its own."

"You're telling me whatever's out there is afraid of you?"

"Yes, *Mu Xitall*. As they should be."

A chill passes over her skin, and without letting her go, I grab the key from around her neck to unlock the refuge. The air is stale and smells of dirt and animal things, but there is a small bed, and it is remote enough to sustain us. At least, for now.

The human male who sought to hurt my female will come, and when he does, I will slaughter him and hang his bones as a warning for the others.

Threaten what is mine, and death will find you.

"I don't guess you happen to have a flashlight, huh?" my female asks, redirecting my murderous thoughts to those of her safety.

Running a claw down my wrist, I reactivate my battle suit, allowing the illuminated fibers that spread across my skin to light the small dwelling.

My female sighs. "Oil lamps. Right. Why would there be electricity?" She wiggles, trying to escape the hold I have on her, and when I don't relent, she meets my gaze. The scent of her arousal rises, teasing my nose. My cock hardens, and my instincts to claim rear to life.

"I should..." she starts, then swallows hard. "I need to..."

"What, *Mu Xitall*? What do you *need*?"

Close enough to taste, her breath comes out heavy—the sweet scent tightening my balls, driving my cock to swell.

A loud wail rings out, and she screams, "Binky!"

Fucking furry overlord, I swear if whatever has taken it does not kill it...

"Do not move," I grind out, then leap from the dwelling to track the infuriating furball through the brush. The loud sound of my female's clumsy footsteps thrash behind me, and I don't know who to throttle first, the damn overlord or my mate.

It screeches again, whining in terror, this time farther away, and when I spot it, the useless creature is cornered by a black fanged beast.

Darkening my battle suit, I dim the lights and prowl toward the predator as it remains distracted by the overlord's cries. It licks its lips in preparation to dine on the tiny overlord's flesh. Stale and sour, the beast reeks of disease. It is dying.

Scaling the tree takes seconds, but the air shifts and reveals my scent. The beast roars loud enough to shake the limbs beneath my feet and lunges at the tiny overlord. I do not hesitate. Catching its jaws in my hands a second before it closes on my mate's beloved creature, I pry them open, ignoring my shredded flesh.

Fear shines in the beast's eyes, and the truth of its intentions are clear. It meant only to feed on the tiny overlord and does not deserve to be sentenced to death. I release it, emulating its growl, giving it one final warning.

If it chooses to advance on me or mine, its fate will be sealed.

Rather than engage, it slinks back into the darkness, hiding beneath the brush. I scoop the tiny overlord in my arms and meet my panic-stricken mate. "What the fuck was that? A panther? There aren't supposed to be panthers here! They're not even native to the islands! Fucking private collectors and animal smugglers and their dick-all regard for wildlife! Where's my girl? Binky, you rotten twat, get over here now."

I now see where the tiny overlord gets its filthy mouth, and to hear such dirty words dance on her tongue...

The furry creature purrs in my arms and offers empty promises inappropriate for a female to offer a mated male—not to mention they are physically impossible. I care not for the creature, but when my female wraps her arms around the damned thing, a fondness stirs.

Useless and taxing as it may be, my mate feels a deep connection to the furball, and so it shall be protected.

"I told you to stay," I say in a low voice, careful to tamp down my frustration. She is here, and her scent consumes my every thought, yet she will not listen and has no concern for her own safety.

She struggles to find footing on the broken ground—her

uncovered feet suffering just as mine have. She kicked off the thin floppy shoes she wore when we first arrived at the shelter. "Yeah, well I've never been good at doing what I'm told."

I snag a claw on the edge of her shirt and pull her close, preparing to lift her, but she resists. "I can walk on my own."

"You are in pain."

"I'm fine."

"Let me help you, *Mu Xitall*. I can feel your discomfort."

"No." Crossing her arms, she stomps through the dark, stumbling and cursing under her breath until I can no longer tolerate her suffering.

"Hey! Put me down!" she yells, stirring the flying things above. I throw her over my shoulder and charge back to the hut. As soon as her feet hit the ground, she jerks the door open and glares at me. "What the hell was that?"

"I could not stand by and watch you hurt yourself any longer." Taking a moment to secure the door, I light the oil lamps and ensure all openings in the tiny hut are sealed.

"You don't get to just do that. I understand you wanted to help, but I needed some space. Today has sucked, and I just wanted a moment to breathe."

A dull ache splinters my rib cage. Space. My mate wanted space *from me*.

With the small room lit enough for my female to see, I take stock of what supplies are available. She will need to eat and sleep, and I will need something to forge weapons. I still have my energy pulse available but without the ability to charge it in my travel pod, I have limited reserves. Despite all attempts at distracting myself, I find Leigh's gaze and stiffen. She is angry with me.

"Well, aren't you going to say anything?"

"I did not want you to suffer as I did, *Mu Xitall*."

"What do you mean *as you did*?" she asks, face stiff and

unyielding. The harsh edges of her mouth turn down when she searches for wounds. "Oh, my God. Saxon, your feet..."

Rushing to a small hole in the corner, she pumps the wet ooze she calls water into a basin and sets it down in front of me. "I'm such an idiot. I didn't even think... Sit, right now! Why didn't you say anything? You carried us all that way, suffering the entire time..."

A fiery pain climbs up my calves as she begins to clean the debris from my ravaged skin. Her lip trembles, and a wetness gathers in the corners of her eyes.

"I've really screwed everything up, haven't I?" she asks between dabs. Drawn to her, I swipe a thumb under her eye and brush away the wetness. "See, and there you go, being all sweet to me again when I've been a such a brat."

"I cannot help it. I was created to ease your suffering."

She stills, and the flicker of the oil lamps dances across her face. "They're going to find us. They're going to try to take you from me."

"Let them come. I do not fear them, *Mu Xitall*."

"You don't understand. Elgin's desperate to make a name for himself and he's planning on using you to do it. He's ruthless and will stop at nothing to get what he wants no matter how many people he has to kill in the process. He's going to try to parade you around like some kind of sideshow and I just can't.... I can't watch them do that to you."

"No one will take you from me or force us apart. Human, Revari, or otherwise. You are mine, *Mu Xitall* and I have waited my entire life for you." The softness of her skin calls to me, and when I reach out to stroke her face, she does not turn away. "To feel you." I drag the rough pad of my thumb across her bottom lip, and lean in, unable to resist. Her lips part, and her breaths shorten. "To taste you."

She wets her lips, and when the pink of her tongue slides

across them I can no longer bear it. Gathering her face in my hands, I press my mouth to hers.

She tastes like forever.

A tiny mewl escapes, driving me forward, and I slide my hands up her curves. She is everything I could ever want, ever dream to have. I see now why the ancient sky spirits sent me to her. No other female could ever make me feel this way.

My hands tangle in her hair, holding her in place while I ravage her mouth, savoring every taste. Her hands wrap around my shoulders, and when she climbs onto my lap, she knocks the basin over, spilling it onto the floor.

"Should I—"

"No, just shut up and kiss me," she commands. Scoring my lip with her teeth, she draws me back in. Pressed flush against me, her hips roll, grinding against my cock with every pulse of her heart.

"Fuck," she mutters against my mouth, spreading her legs wider and increasing her speed. Her arousal seeps through the fabric of her pants, spilling onto my own, and something inside me shifts.

Desire. Need. The dark craving to slide into her naked flesh and have her scream my name—the emotions overtake me and I can see nothing but her.

Snagging her shirt with my claws, I rip it off, baring her breasts with a growl, and pull the first little peak into my mouth and suck. Hard.

"Oh, shit," she squeaks out as I flip her over and lay her underneath me. Her pale cheeks are reddened with arousal and she arches in the most delicious way when I pull the other hard nub into my mouth. "What are you doing with your tongue—oh fuck. Whatever, keep going."

She moans again, writhing underneath me, rubbing her sex

against my cock in long strokes. She is eager and soaked, and I am going to enjoy every second of this.

"I want to see you, *Mu Xitall*. All of you." Her pants slip off easily, and as she lifts her hips to meet my cock once again, I squeeze her clit between my fingers and press her hips back down.

Her body is unlike a Revari female's, but it feels as if I've already memorized every curve.

"Not yet. I want to drink you in and taste the sweetness you offer me. "

Shoving her arms over her head, I lock them in place with a firm grip. She will not be allowed to touch. She will feel what I give her, what I provide and nothing else.

Tracing her skin with the tip of my claw, I drag it down between her breasts and wait for her to squirm beneath my touch.

That's right, mate. *Writhe for me.*

"Saxon," she mutters, lifting up to meet my lips, and I cannot deny her. Grinding my hips with each stroke of my tongue, I drink her in, cherishing the way she fights to get closer. My cock strains against my pants, but I do not dare take her.

Not yet. Not until I have claimed every inch of her body will I claim her soul.

She whimpers in protest when I pull away, and the separation is almost too much. It's like my soul shatters the further I am from her warmth, and it will not be fully healed until I am balls deep inside her.

"Tell me what you would like, *Mu Xitall*," I demand, scoring my teeth along the curve of her hips. She shutters under my tongue as I drag the tip closer and closer to her heat and nip at the inside of her thigh.

"You, fuck. I want you."

With a flick of my tongue, all conscious thought is lost. *Mine.* She screams, gulping for air as I ravage her tender flesh.

Delving in with hot, wet strokes, I suck her into my mouth, scraping my teeth along her swollen nub. "Please," she cries, fighting against my hold. She's soaked for me, dripping with need, and no matter how many times I lap up her nectar, it will never be enough.

I am going to fucking devour her.

Her hips buck in time with her moans and she's dug her heels into the fabric beneath us, thrusting her sex against my tongue.

"So sweet, so succulent, *Mu Xitall.* You will never come for another," I warn, sliding a finger inside her. Her walls stretch for me, greeting me like they too recognize me for what I am.

"I just want to come for you. Please, I can't take it," she whines, suffocating my next words with her softness. Caught off guard, I lighten my hold and she breaks free.

A deep growl escapes as she grips my hair with both hands and yanks me up, forcing my mouth to hers. She rips at my pants, struggling to free my cock, and when she wraps her hands around my length, I snap.

With a roar, I slam my cock into her, nearly splitting her in two. Her face twists up, and just as I start to relent, she tightens her knees and begins to whimper.

Something incomprehensible tears from her lips, and she drags her nails down my spine while I pump in and out of her, balls slapping against her ass. The scent of our arousal swirls in the air, driving me forward, and with each stroke, she tightens her hold and begs for more.

Leaning up, I angle my hips, meeting the unquenchable demand to drive into her harder, faster until her high-pitched moans turn hoarse. She grips my shoulders and grunts, her cries increasing faster and faster until I feel her body clench and shudder around me.

Pumping into her with one last stroke, I empty my seed inside of her, gripping her thighs and pushing until my cock can go no further. She cries out a final time and I swallow her moans with a tender kiss.

Her skin—slick with sweat—shines like the stars in the dim light, and I cannot help but stare. She is beautiful.

"That was...holy crap, there aren't even words for how amazing that was," she manages between pants. "I've never..." She moves the loose strands of hair from my face. "You're amazing, you know that? And you're so hot and thoughtful and damn it, I don't know how to do this. "

"You do not need to explain, *Mu Xitall*. I feel what you feel," I say pressing my hand to her chest. Her heart stutters under my palm.

She swipes her hand down her face and lifts her gaze. "It doesn't make sense. I don't understand how I can feel *so much* for you after so little time. And now after what we just did, shit. And how you just flipped my world upside down? I don't know what this is, but I'm terrified of losing it."

Her lips tremble, and I ease them with a kiss, then place another on her brow. I do not understand. She mourns our bond like it is lost, and it has only begun.

CHAPTER EIGHT

Leigh

Saxon's gaze holds mine, but he doesn't say anything. Did I reveal too much? I've never been the type to swoon over sex, but he just turned me inside out four times over and I swear, if he so much as shifts his hips we're going another round.

I can't get enough of him. Whatever he's inspired inside me has knocked me on my ass and left me completely off kilter. I've never been in love. Never found a man I wanted more than I wanted to achieve my goals, and now he's here staring me right in the face and I'm flopping in the wind completely ungrounded.

The ends of his hair tease my collarbone as he braces his weight on the arm of the couch and hovers over me. Shining like a beacon to my soul, his golden eyes search mine.

Say something—anything—and tell me I haven't completely lost my mind.

"Have I told you the story of my arrival, *Mu Xitall?*" he

asks, nudging my nose then pressing his lips to mine. My core heats as his tongue pushes its way into my mouth.

His cock sits heavy against my thigh, and it's taking every-thing in me not to reach for him and avoid this conversation all together. Why is this stuff so hard? Why can't I just talk about my emotions like a normal person?

"All births are celebrated on Revaris, but none more than a child born under a Xisun Moon. It is a time where our twin moons align, and the ancient sky spirits are said to speak the loudest. I was one of twelve young born that night, and when I matured, I was marked as an Exune.

"Revaris is a small planet, and though we excel in strength and combat, we cannot solely breed within our own race. It weakens our power. We need diversity to thrive—to constantly meet the needs of our species to adapt. Introducing new beings into life on Revaris is crucial to our survival.

"On the eve of our maturity, at the time that marks our birth, the ancient sky spirits reveal our mates in the form of a vision, and the few selected Exune meant to travel the stars to find the one for them receive a mark like this."

Saxon turns his head and pulls back his ear to reveal a cres-cent shaped moon. "We are offered no explanation of why we were chosen, and unlike the others, we are given no hint of who it is we are meant to find. Just the promise that when we do, we will know without question."

Unable to control my face, my brow furrows. "That seems so unfair. I mean, what happens if you don't find her?"

"An Exune will look until his last breath." Letting his lips tease mine, Saxon smiles against my mouth. "Or until she finds him."

The amusement on his face is contagious, and I smile. "I did find you, huh?"

"You did, *Mu Xitall*. And you have continued to save me

every moment since."

"You saved me, too. You know that? And not just from the water..." I say, voice cracking with emotion. Damn, I hate that I'm such a sap with him, but I can't help it. We're stuck in a hut in the middle of nowhere with half of the world chasing us by now, and all I want to do is wrap myself in his arms and hide away. We're going to have to run. He's going to have to leave, and I'm just not ready.

I don't think I'll ever be.

"We saved each other, and now you too, bear my mark. If you ever question the reality of our connection, it is now etched in your skin just as you are etched into my soul."

My hand goes to the back of my ear, and I gasp. Tiny raised lines in the very same shape. But wait, if his story is real then...

"You really aren't worried about Elgin, are you? Because... you want to take me back there, to Revaris."

He stiffens, worry tightening his smile. "It is my hope. But without the ability to raise the other Revari males, I do not know the functionality of my pod. It is made to carry two, but I spent so long buried in the liquid prison..."

Panic tightens my throat. "Saxon, the other males. Now that Elgin knows you're alive..."

"Do not worry. Their pods will not register on your technology. But, I cannot lie to you, *Mu Xitall*. Now, that I have tasted what it is like to share my existence with another I cannot sentence them to a life spent alone—forever trapped with only dreams of their mate to sustain them. They will not survive for much longer. The pods will not keep them alive them indefinitely."

My heart breaks for him. Knowing that his people are down there and we're here. What if he can't get them out? Or worse, what if they're already dead? He looks away and clenches his jaw. There's something else...

"What is it, Saxon? Whatever it is, tell me. We're in this together. "

"My brother... He too, lies sleeping in the liquid prison."

"Oh, shit. What can we do? I mean—"

Saxon presses a finger to my lips, silencing me. "Get dressed, *Mu Xitall*. An enemy approaches," he whispers and slides from between my legs.

As he swipes a claw across his wrist, black ripples out from the wound and spreads across his skin, covering him. His eyes darken, claws extend, and for the first time in the light I see why the animals in the forest were afraid.

He's fucking terrifying, and like all deadly things, absolutely beautiful.

I grab Binky, praying that for once she knows when to shut up and behave, while Saxon snuffs out the lights. We've been here less than two hours. How did they find us already?

The boom of my heart in my ears is deafening. It's pitch black, and I can't see anything at all. Voices echo through the small window near the door. Footsteps trample the sticks, getting louder by the second, and I swallow the panic threatening to choke me.

The air stirs behind me, and I can feel his breath on my face. "Fear not, I am here and I will never leave you."

I reach out to touch him for some semblance of comfort but he's gone. Where is he? And more importantly, who the hell is here?

A slight breeze slinks into the room. Wait, that window wasn't open before...

Tiptoeing to the window, I sink underneath out of sight and press my back to the wall.

Binky hisses as someone passes by outside. Soldiers. More than one from the sound of their voices. I can't make out what they're saying, no matter how hard I listen, but it doesn't take a genius to figure out they're looking for us. Why else would they be all the way out here?

The night falls silent again until a muted scream ignites the forest in animal chatter.

No! Saxon! Clutching Binky to my chest, I slap a hand over my mouth to smother my urge to call out for him. I swear if I don't hear from him soon, I'm finding the first sharp thing I can and going out there to get him.

Big scary alien or not, he's mine and no one's taking him from me.

Several screams ring out in the distance, along with a blood-curdling growl, but before I make it to the door to find him, Saxon's there, chest heaving. I rush forward and wrap my arms around him as his suit retracts back into his wrist.

"What...what happened? Were those soldiers out there? I mean, I thought maybe the local public safety officers would be looking for us but not a bunch of guys with guns."

He holds me closer, tightening his arms, and presses a kiss to my forehead. "I did not have time to interrogate them, *Mu Xitall*, but the voice on the communication device strapped to their vests spoke of searching something called a forest for us." He lets out a deep growl. "They did not get the chance to reveal their findings."

"Where are they? What did you do to them?"

"Do not trouble yourself with the filth of battle. Only know that the black beast of the forest will bother the tiny overlord no more. Her belly is full."

It takes me a few seconds to really digest what he says, and even then, I can't believe it.

"Holy crap, you *fed* them to the panther? This is all really happening, huh?"

"Those males... They were outfitted to kill, not detain. We need to keep moving, *Mu Xitall*."

Binky purrs and hops down to rub her face on his leg like he just killed those guys in her honor. Really? Freaking harlot.

"Where? Where will we go? This is the only place I could think of that we'd be safe. Elgin has a contract with the US military on Guam. Those must be his guys. We can't go there or any of the other islands if he's got an army on his payroll. The travel here is limited in and out, and everyone goes through a screening process. There's nowhere for us to go."

"Do not—" Faint but unmistakable, a whistling noise zings toward us.

"Saxon? What is it?"

He stiffens for a split second, then he hits the ground with a thud.

"No!" I scream and lunge for him, feeling all over his body for a wound. Nothing on his head, chest, face... I don't understand. What's happening? Why isn't he responding?

"Saxon... Saxon... Wake up!" I grab his face, turning it toward me, but when I let go, it flops to the floor. Shaking him does nothing. "Okay, think, Leigh," I mumble in a frenzied panic, then check his pulse. Strong and steady, his heart's beating. He's breathing in and out, what could be—

Footsteps. Light and muffled. Nowhere near as loud as the heavy ones from before.

Whoever it is scurries closer, and I grab the nearest oil lamp. It's not much but it's still hot, and whoever comes through that door is getting it smashed right into their face.

They get closer, and I suck in a deep breath trying to steady my hand. I'm standing over Saxon, straddling him, when a draft blows through the open door, and a giant shadow flies into the room.

I raise the lamp, curling it behind me ready to smash it into the intruder's face when she steps into the cabin and clicks on a light.

CHAPTER NINE

Leigh

"Anya? What the fuck? Why do you have a house plant on your head?"

She shoves me away from Saxon and turns to close the door. "Get back. You don't have to pretend anymore. You're safe. By the time he wakes up, we'll be long gone."

Her muddy feet slap against the worn floor when she pads over and rips out a dart from the back of his shoulder. She lets out a low whistle and runs her hand over his wrist. "What have we here?"

Anya pulls out a tiny metal scanner and waves it over him. "Inconclusive? That's not right. This thing detects any known element. Holy shit. He's not even human. Super soldiers? They've got fucking super soldiers now? What have you gotten yourself into, girl?"

"Me? First of all, what the hell did you shoot him with? He better not die, Anya, or I'm going to kick your ass."

She lowers her messy, leaf-covered hood and unzips her

camouflage jacket. "Oh, calm your tits, Leigh. It's my special concoction. There's only a tiny bit curare in there. He'll be fine. And since when do you care about saving your captor. You have Stockholm syndrome or something?"

"Curare!" I yell out, and she motions for me to lower my voice. "That kills people. Why the hell did you dart him anyway? You're the worst stalker ever. If you'd been following me correctly, you'd have seen he went out there to save my life."

Her eyes widen, and she throws her hands on her hips. "Oh, you mean when he slaughtered the three soldiers? With his bare hands? Yeah, saw that. Didn't know you were playing for the same team."

"Well, maybe you would have if you weren't freaking hiding in the bushes in a damn leaf suit!"

"You didn't see me did you?" she asks with more attitude than I appreciate. I don't bother to respond, so she continues, peering out the window, searching for threats. "The last time we spoke, you sounded off. Then you suddenly disappeared mid-conversation like you were being kidnapped off your boat! I've spent hours searching the radio waves for a clue, and once I heard the dispatch to search the woods from those military goons stationed on Guam, I tracked you here. To save you."

She sighs and shakes her head. "Some nerve you've got, yelling at me like this. I missed dinner. Not to mention exposing myself to all the damn cameras between here and my place. I think I deserve a little appreciation." Anya's frizzy silver french braid hangs loose over her shoulder as she sinks down into a crouch to pull a knife out of her boot.

Saxon stirs, and Anya jumps to her feet. "Impossible, there's no way he could wake up that fast."

I sigh and sink down beside her. "You're right. He's couldn't...if he were human."

After taking a long swig from the canteen strapped to her

side, she looks at me. "I knew it! Where'd he escape from? I figured this island had a research facility, but I've never been able to figure out its location. "

She mumbles to herself for several seconds before my patience thins. "Stop! He's not a damn government project or a super soldier or a war machine. He's just a man I found at the bottom of the trench in some sort of ship right before I nearly died. He saved me. He'd been trapped down there for who knows how long. I guess I woke him up."

She pauses a moment while her mind connects the dots. "So, he's an alien. But then why's the military searching for you...? Ah, shit. Elgin wants him doesn't he?"

I nod and slide to the floor beside him. His skin's clammy, I'm guessing from the poison, so I swipe the sweat from his brow and press a kiss to his forehead. The vein in his neck still pulses, and his breathing is relaxed. "Yes. Both of us. Not only is he framing me for stealing money, Elgin installed a secret camera in Henrietta and has been watching me for months. He saw the whole thing. He wants Saxon as payment for destroying her."

"Shadowy bastards. Not on my watch. Don't worry about the video. I can take care of that. As for the frame job, we can figure that out, too. Help me get him up." Anya squats, grabbing Saxon's arm and trying to hoist him over her shoulder. "Good gods, what does this guy eat? He weighs at least two-eighty," she says, struggling.

Well, I can name one thing, but it wasn't exactly nutritious...

Binky howls as I grab my bag and shove her inside, leaving only a small gap in the zipper at the top for her to breathe. Flipping it around so it hangs against my chest, I slide underneath Saxon's other arm, and together we start off through the trees.

"You going to tell me where we're going or what?" I manage

through gritted teeth. She's right, Saxon's heavy as hell, and carrying him requires me to tense every single muscle I have, and some I didn't even know existed. But if it keeps him safe...

"I've got a place near here, but if I'm going to take you there, we need to do this right. Stop here. I'm going to go back and hide our tracks. They're always watching, Leigh. Always waiting for me to screw up. The second I do, they'll find me."

Right. Again with the paranoid delusions and shadow men. Usually, this is the part where I start to tune out, but this time, I'm actually paying attention. I love Anya, and she's special in her own way, but she gets to be a little much. I mean, she poisoned my man with a blow dart for fuck's sake. Who even uses those anymore?

Let me answer that. No one. Because it's insane. But then again, I thought people who believed in little green men hiding on Earth were too.

Every twenty minutes, we stop, and I sag to the ground, taking a completely limp Saxon with me while Anya dashes off looking like a hillbilly Christmas tree to hide our footsteps and whatever else she thinks we need to do to keep someone from following.

He's been in and out like he's sweating off a fever, and he keeps mumbling in a language I've never heard. He's going to be so pissed when he wakes up and realizes what's happened.

The muscles in my neck are on fire, my mouth's dry, and just before my legs give out, Anya gives me the signal to stop.

"All right," she says, tightening her long-sleeved camo coat. "We're close, this should be the last time." With silent steps, she follows our footprints back without missing a beat, using only the moon's silvery light to guide her.

It's hot as hell out here. Humid too. I have no idea how she hasn't passed out by now. I'm in nothing but the tank and shorts I managed to throw on and I swear I'm about to pass out.

Saxon's long locks are splayed out across my legs as I cradle his head. He's growling in his sleep, like he's fighting to wake. Every once in a while he manages to throw out an arm or leg, and I have to fight to keep hold of him.

After dousing one of the shirts I packed with water from my canteen, I dab his forehead. The hard lines of his face relax under my touch, and I stare at him. The second I heard him hit the ground, my heart sped into overdrive and I haven't been able to calm it since. It feels like if I look away, he'll stop breathing and I'll lose him forever.

If I was confused at all before about my feelings, I'm not now. I don't care if it makes sense or not, Saxon belongs with me. Everything else, I'll figure out later. All I've done my entire life is try to prove to other people who I am and who I'm not. With him, I just want to *be*.

Using the dim light on my watch, I time his breathing again. Then his heart rate. I don't understand why he won't wake up. He's been asleep now for over an hour, and the longer he stays unconscious, the darker my thoughts turn. What if he never wakes up? What if I finally found someone who makes me feel, but lose him without ever really knowing him?

CHAPTER TEN

Saxon

My fucking arms won't work, nor my legs. Left to flop help-lessly while my female and her strange friend bear my weight angers me more by the second. I'm created to protect her, yet this tiny human in a ridiculous forest suit dropped me on my ass in half a second.

How'd she do it? And why has my female not challenged her?

On my planet, if another female had done the same, there would be blood. And justly so. The mate bond is volatile and does not take kindly to those who seek to break it. We are raised to protect life, but even the most patient of us would seek to avenge this.

Laughter echoes in the recesses of my mind. "Perhaps, your female knew of your need for a good thrashing."

Pavil! He wakes! Joy and relief thrum through me at the sound of my brother's voice inside my mind, but I will not reveal it. If I speak truthfully he will never stop reminding me.

Near death or not, my stubborn need to triumph over him will not yield.

"Mind your tongue, you nosey bastard, and tell me how you have awakened. I thought I would have to come down and pull you out myself."

"Come now, brother. You cannot be that dense. I was forced awake by your instinctive cry for help. Our blood connection demanded I respond."

"I did no such thing," I reply. He laughs again, this time slightly louder than the last. I can feel the distance between us changing. "You are in motion…and closer to me than before."

"Well, you cannot wake me in such a dreary place and expect me not to thoroughly explore it. My travel pod was unable to calculate the time we have been on this planet, and the exterior shows immense wear. Not to mention my inability to reach Cyfer and Ajax.

"Why would the ancients bother to send us here? The pressure in this spirit-forsaken place is nearly unbearable. You cannot even maintain a stiff cock long enough to mate. Not to mention, it's dark and the creatures here…they are tiny. There's no way I would fit—"

"Pavil…"

The gentle caress of my mate's hand on my face stops, and I'm once again hoisted into her arms. As the sting of the poison lessens, I feel my strength returning, and the pull to wake grows stronger. I fight against it, letting the poison continue to ravage my veins for a few minutes more. My mate's heart races, and the scent of her fear thickens the air, but I cannot maintain this connection with Pavil while awake.

"What? No offense to your female, Saxon. But this planet sucks. Put me back to sleep. At least there I wouldn't feel like my brain is going to squeeze through my ears."

"You haven't even made it to the surface, you idiot! You have yet to see an Earth female."

"Earth? Is that where we are? What a disappointing name for a planet." The insufferable hint of laughter that always resides in his voice dies. "Brother, I can feel your panic. All joking aside, are you harmed?"

"Not yet. But I am being hunted."

Pavil laughs. "Who would be dense enough to hunt a Revari male? Do these Earth beings not know of our abilities? Our brute strength?"

"They know nothing, brother. They do not travel the stars. This is not the same universe we set off in. The great blackhole threw us into a different time. An older, more primitive one."

"You're serious?" he asks, caution stiffening his tone. For once in his life, he's managed to grasp the gravity of our situation without me having to hold him down and beat it into him.

"I am. Several human males have already tried and failed to capture us. Their shredded remains stain the ground, but there are others and we have little time."

Something cool slides across my forehead, and warm, salt-filled droplets slide down my face. Tears...but they are not my own. My female...she mourns, and I cannot ignore the pull to comfort her.

"Stay alive, asshole. I am coming..." Pavil calls out as our connection weakens. He tugs hard on the bond that connects us, that my body activated while unconscious, and it recoils, fighting against his will.

"Do not come for me. Find our travel pods first and wake the others. We will need them at full strength if we are to get the fuck out of this place without burning it to the ground."

Leigh

Once we make it to the edge of the trees, Anya leaves me to shoulder Saxon's weight and then scans the area with night vision goggles. "We're clear," she says, scurrying over to a pile of brush. Where are we?

A tiny illuminated keypad appears once she's displaced a large branch and after entering an impossibly long code, it opens up to reveal a set of stairs.

What the...? Seriously?

As she passes through the steel entrance, a red laser scans her face.

"All right, let's go. The drones fly overhead every four hours. By my count, that gives us less than five minutes to get him inside before they make their rounds. Hurry up. That door's closing whether you're inside or not."

"Holy shit. You really are a spy," I manage while trying to hoist Saxon off the ground. Anya watches me struggle for a second before sighing loudly. I don't know why I'm so surprised. I guess after all the crazy stuff I've heard her say, I never actually considered that she could be telling the truth.

"I swear you're single handedly going to deliver me to the United States government," she mutters as she hurries back and curls an arm around his. "And for the record, I tried to tell you."

My muscles tremble under the strain of Saxon's weight, but I clench my teeth until we've cleared the stairs. I collapse on the floor with him as soon as the door slams shut. The sounds of heavy bolts sliding into place echo through the metal-lined walls, and Anya drops down alongside me.

"No, you didn't! You just said a bunch of nonsense that made me think you were a crazy ole coot who'd spent too much time sniffing dirty air in the restricted zone."

She unzips the top of her camouflage suit and slides it off

her sweat drenched arms. A laugh bubbles up at the sight of her *Breakfast Club* t-shirt. Her thick salt and pepper eyebrows draw in. "How flattering. Here I was thinking we were friends who were mutually interested in maintaining the others' survival."

Ah, hell. I hurt her feelings. Good job, Leigh. Way to pay your friend back for risking her life. I pull Saxon's sweaty palm into my lap and mindlessly rub his fingers. "I didn't mean it like that. I appreciate your help. And I do...you know, care about your survival. After you spend all day talking to machine parts, you forget how to talk to real people. I just suck at being a friend." I shrug, not knowing what else to say.

She stands, then pulls out a semi-automatic machine gun from the side of her camo onesie. Where the hell was she hiding that? "Yeah, so do I. Come on. We need to see how much shit we've stirred up."

My legs give out when I try to lift Saxon again, and no matter how many times I try, my muscles refuse to cooperate. I'm totally prepared to curl up next to him on the floor, but Anya shakes her head and stalks away. After rolling Saxon onto one of her tarps, we slide him down a narrow hall into what she calls her command room.

Turns out her "place" is really a two-level underground shelter abandoned after the tsunami flattened that part of the island. You'd think after being left to sink back into the earth, its internal structure would be a little worse for the wear, but no. She's got so much tech in here it's making my head spin. I still can't get over the fact she's really an ex-spook.

Making sure to cover Saxon's bare chest, I prop his head on a blanket after checking his vitals again. It's been a little over an hour and a half, and he's still in and out.

"Stop messing with him. He'll be fine," Anya mutters while pouring some water from a bottle into a bowl. Binky glares at me, still pissed about the whole shoving her inside a backpack thing, then trots over to drink.

She's lucky I didn't leave her furry little ass in the trees.

"I can't help it. It's really freaking me out. Are we good? Any more of those pricks closing in?"

A side sweeping camera view of the area surrounding the shelter pops up on the twenty screens lining her wall, and she grabs one of fifty spiral notebooks on her desk and starts to take notes. "Everything's stable for now. Activity patterns haven't changed. Elgin's likely still waiting for a report of tonight's failure. But they won't stop coming. Men like him never do."

Anya's chair squeaks when she swivels toward where I'm sitting. "Oh, for fuck's sake. Stop looking like an abused puppy. If he was going to die, he'd have done it by now. If the bastard's as smart as I think he is, he's probably already awake, waiting for the perfect moment to hop up and slit my throat."

My mouth drops open in shock. "You're serious..."

"Wouldn't be the first time," she says, shrugging her shoulders and looking strangely comfortable with the notion of someone trying to murder her.

She has a point...

I give his dick a little nudge, hopeful it's all a façade, but I get nothing. No way he's pretending. The last time I got anywhere near that massive thing he nearly split me in two with it.

"Nah, he's still out and he looks terrible. Isn't there anything you can give him? You did poison him after all..."

"It just has to run its course. You both look like hell, and you, especially, need to sleep. You sure you feel safe with him?" she asks, searching my eyes for even the slightest hint of deceit. After tucking the blanket around him once more, I meet her gaze.

"I do." Anya narrows her eyes. "Look, I know it doesn't make sense and I can't explain it, but I know he won't hurt me."

"All right, then. I'll set you up in the safe room..." She hesitates a moment, then clears her throat. "It's the only place without cameras. Plus, if those assholes make it in here, I'm dead anyway. At least this way you'll have enough rations for a few weeks and you can die on your own terms. No way anyone's getting through those doors once they're locked tight unless you or I want them too."

She pads over to a metal cabinet and wrenches its rusted doors open to grab a thick black clip. "Here. You can hook this up to his finger and it will monitor his oxygen and his heart. Hit the comm button on the wall and call for me if either change significantly. Make sure not to hit anything else. That room can double as a cell, and I'd hate for you to lock yourself in."

After placing a blanket around my shoulders, she gives them a squeeze. "It's not like we have an alien health manual. But I'm guessing if he stays the same, he'll wake up just fine."

"Yeah. He has to. He will." Now, if I could only convince my head to shut the hell up, I might actually believe it.

CHAPTER ELEVEN

Leigh

As soon as the lights turn off, I'm left with nothing but an unconscious alien lover and my thoughts and, holy shit, there are a lot of them. Let's be real, self-reflection hasn't ever really been my thing. I'm more of a take action and think about the consequences later kind of girl, but now with Saxon...

I worry about him. He hasn't woken up. I'm exhausted and dirty but I can't bring myself to sleep until I hear his voice. The thin pallet Anya rolled out for us barely blunts the hardness of the concrete floor. My hip burns, but I'm too tired to care. The last thirty-six hours have been the most intense of my life and I don't know what to do.

Under any other circumstances, I'd run. I have a little cash put up, enough for me to pay someone under the table to leave the island, but there's no way I could hide Saxon.

I don't really know what passed between us the moment we met, but whatever it was changed me forever. I can't leave him.

If you'd have asked me five years ago what was most important in my life, it would have been me. It's a shitty thing to say, but it's reality. My entire life I've felt the need to prove that I'm more than what everyone expected me to be. I created Henrietta. I made it to the deepest part of the ocean. And now?

The most important thing to me is him opening those fucking sunshine eyes, and the fact that he hasn't makes my heart bleed.

Another tear falls, wetting his clammy cheek, and I rest my forehead against his. "Hey, I need you to wake up. I really suck at all this emotional shit and I need you."

The absolute silence inside Anya's saferoom is deafening. I want to give in and expel all the emotions twisting me into knots, but I can't afford to fall apart. Not until he's better. Not until he's really with me.

The air conditioner kicks on, and a cool burst of air snakes its way through the room. A chill spreads across Saxon's skin, so I wrap my arms around him and rest my head on his shoulder.

He's been shirtless since Anya darted him, and I don't want him to be cold. My breath is hot against his neck, and no matter how close I snuggle, it's not enough.

With heavy lids, I start to drift—my mind seeking a less tempestuous reality but right as my thoughts finally fade, two words have me hurtling back to the present.

"*Mu Xitall.*" His voice is raw, like the mention of my name brings forth such emotion he can hardly form the sounds.

"Saxon—" Warm lips swallow my reply, and then he's on me. I tear my mouth from his to caress his face. "Are you okay? I thought you were—oh!" I moan, writhing against the warm fingers he's slid inside me. Crashing back against his lips, I fumble with the seamless waist of his pants, and he withdraws his fingers to pull down my shorts.

"Mine," he mutters between harsh breaths as he bares himself.

Intertwining our fingers, Saxon slides into me with one rough thrust, and fuck, it hurts and feels so good at the same time. The twinge of soreness from our first time warms, climbing its way up my spine and hitting me hard in the chest. Tears once again burn my eyes, and with each slow stroke of Saxon's cock, I'm held captive by an overwhelming mixture of ecstasy and gratitude that he's safe and alive.

"I missed you," he whispers in my ear, slowing his pace. Every inch of him slides back and forth with intention, like he's savoring every sensation. His strong hands wrap around my shoulders, guiding me up and onto his lap so that I'm sitting on him.

I wrap him in a tight embrace, and we hold each other. He grips my thighs, lifting me up and down with ease, and as he fills me completely over and over, a sense of finality settles into place. He's it for me. No matter what, we'll figure this out.

The buck of his hips and the thumb he rubs along my clit send me over the edge, and I cry out with him deep inside me. He grunts with one last thrust, and we both collapse on the pallet.

I hate that I can't see him. I know he's right here, but with no light, it still feels like he's so far away.

Damn, when did I get so emotional?

His skin's warm to the touch now and I lie on his chest, keeping him close. "Forgive me for my absence, my Leigh," he says, helping me slide my shorts up.

"Why are you apologizing? It's not like you asked Anya to dart you."

Saxon chuckles, and presses a kiss to my cheek. "Ah, that is the human female's name. I do not care for her methods of protecting you, but the sentiment does not go unnoticed. I cannot stay angry with someone who cares for you as I do."

"She really does. Care about me, I mean. She just does it in her own way."

"Her way is cumbersome, inconvenient, and my tolerance of her methods has expired. But I cannot deny its efficacy. It is an easy thing to love you, *Mu Xitall*. There is nothing I would not do to keep you safe. I expect no less from those you surround yourself with.

"My ire with her stems from what would have occurred if more soldiers were to have arrived and she was unable to protect you herself."

My fingers dance along the strong muscles of his shoulders, and I cringe when I reach the tiny spot where the dart was and feel the swelling. It hasn't healed for some reason. There must still be some residual poison in it. "Hey, I'm fine. Right? We're both okay. But I don't ever want to do that again."

He chuckles. "Perhaps, we should ensure your human friend is aware of your preferences."

"Oh, she knows. I was so pissed when she charged in there like a psychotic Mother Earth. But then she took us here to keep us safe once she figured out what was going on. This is her place, and it's a big deal for her to let someone in."

"This dwelling. It is secured?" Saxon asks. "I cannot sense anyone outside of your human companion. And even then, her scent is faint."

Shifting on the hard ground, I opt for lying flat on my stomach to give my hips and back a break. Almost as if he can sense my discomfort, Saxon pulls me mostly on top of him, and I melt against his chest.

"Yeah," I mumble, already being pulled under by the lull of my exhaustion. My man's safe. I'm safe. And in this moment, that's all that matters. "This place is locked up tight like Fort Knox. Oh, and Anya's not crazy, after all. She's a spy. Forgot to mention that."

My head tingles in the most wonderful way as Saxon threads his fingers through the strands and massages my scalp. "I suspected this much. Rest now, my Leigh. You strained your body too much carrying me here."

I mean to tell him how bossy he is, how it's not like I had a choice, but when he starts to hum *Clare De Lune*, all conscious thought is lost and I fall into darkness.

CHAPTER TWELVE

Saxon

"I was wondering when you'd come. Took you longer than I suspected. She still passed out?" the one called Anya asks, calling me from the shadows. As soon as my Leigh was deep in sleep, I exited the room via the ventilation system to scout.

I need to ensure my mate and I are safe here and the security measures in place are sufficient. Anya does not know of our kind's ability to disconnect our joints to allow for smooth passage though small spaces. If not for that ability, the pressure in the wet ooze alone would have ended me.

"She is."

"Ducts? Or did you override the key panel and disarm the motion sensors?" she asks, seated in front of several large illuminated screens. They appear to be some kind of rudimentary processing machines. Back on Revaris, everything is connected to the chips placed in our brain. You sync, you think, it happens. Here there is the necessity to punch tiny buttons to spell out each word and wait for the thing to respond.

How tedious and time consuming.

When I don't answer, she taps a few of the buttons on the machine to her right. Several red lines flash on the screen then turn green.

"Computer says the sensors are all intact. The ducts then. Surprised you could fit. Guess I should have considered that before I put you in there."

Suddenly, the female jumps from her chair, and in one smooth motion pulls a long barrel weapon from underneath a nearby table. A loud crack resonates through the room when she cocks it.

"This is not necessary—"

"Speak for yourself," she says, then slams her hand down on a red lever. The lights go out, and we're left in total darkness.

Shaking my head, I engage my battle suit. Humans. Do they not realize an elevated species can see in the dark? Like with many things on this planet, I do not understand the point of this. Is it a sparring session? Some sort of competition? Surely, she does not believe she can overpower me.

Again.

Pavil's annoying laughter echoes in the back of my head. Of course, my mind would summon the sound knowing the female has, in fact, overpowered me once. Wherever he is, he better be following my orders. I need to get my mate off this spirit-forsaken planet before I'm forced to massacre an entire army to save her. And myself. Something I will not hesitate to do if forced.

The human female dives around the corner, and I advance, slowly, keeping low to the ground. The smell of her excitement and fear triggers my instincts, and my claws lengthen. Veins swell with the urge to hunt, and my pupils widen. I want to give in, allow my instincts to consume my mind and hunt her like I did those males in the woods.

Revari males are carnivores with an instinctual drive to provide for the females and young of their tribe. We fight, protect, and kill to feed our people. But we are also raised to protect life if at all possible.

Giving in would allow a more volatile side of me to escape, and I would not be in complete control of my aggression. I cannot harm her. Not after everything she has done for me and my mate. She is part of my female's tribe and, as such, should be protected.

The familiar whistle of those cumbersome darts rings out in the distance and I roll to the side, narrowly avoiding them. Up on my feet, I press myself against a metal cabinet and wait for her to approach. Her steps may be muffled, but they are loud to my ears, and I can count the number until she comes within arm's reach.

It really is a wonder she was able to catch me unaware before. In hindsight, the safety of my mate in that moment consumed me. Her beauty, her scent—just the gift of her existence commands my attention. I will need to do better in the future.

Anya sneaks closer, the same familiar heavy metal weapon causing her to displace weight on her right.

"You may lower your weapon. I do not wish to harm you."

She positions the weapon and laughs. "Right, and I'm an alien from outer space. Oh, wait. That's you. So, no thanks. I'm going to tie you up, then figure out what to do with you."

Her eyes are wild and bloodshot. Exhaustion has darkened the skin underneath. She has expended a great amount of energy trying to find and rescue my Leigh. My annoyance with her softens, however it will remain as long as the hole in my fucking back. Her insistence on playing this little game does not make it any better.

"We do not have time for this nonsense." Shifting too fast for her to register, I rip the dart propeller from around her neck, leaving the weapon in her hand alone, and crush it. Then I dive behind a metal partition.

"Aw, man. What the fuck? That took me months to carve. What that really necessary?"

I let out a huff. "You expected something less? That makes twice you have attempted to kill me."

"Damn it. I didn't expect you to be that fast."

"I would apologize, but to be honest, I do not give a shit. Now tell me, those males chasing us. Who are they?"

"I'm not saying nothin' until you come out from behind that wall. I'm not new to this game, boy, let me see you." She motions me forward with the barrel of her weapon, and even though I know the ammunition cannot pierce my suit, I offer up my hands in submission. The seeing contraption on her face has a strange gleam to the lenses when she finally finds me in the dark.

Her chest is puffed out in confidence and her shoulders have relaxed. She does not realize it, but she has gotten too close. The ancient weapon in her hands has given her a false confidence, that if I chose to act would lead to her doom.

However, she will remain unharmed. I will tolerate her, as I do the furry overlord—from a distance and in small doses.

Wait, *damn it*. Where is the wretched creature? I can scent it. Hear the faint beat of its heart. Surely, it has been fed. My Leigh will not be pleased.

"There you are. Keep those claws where I can see 'em," Anya warns, holding me in her sights. I maintain my hands in a raised position and walk forward three steps. "Fuck, you're more impressive awake. Starting to second guess my game plan here."

"The furry overlord, Bink. Where is she? Has she been maintained?"

"Holy shit, Leigh sure has you trained, don't she? The little brat is the next room over, bathing in a mound of catnip. She's fine. It's you I want to talk about. Now, I know my friend likes you—loves you, even—but I'm not about to let you whisk her off into the sunset or wherever the fuck you're plannin' to go without knowing every single detail about you."

My jaw tightens, and my nostrils flare. How dare she demand something of me when she has already wasted my time and attempted to poison me. "Choose your words carefully, female. My patience wears thin. I will answer your questions but I require your respect in return. Lower your weapon."

She chews on her lip, then groans. "Damn it, Leigh. If you get me killed," she mutters to herself. "The armor you're wearing...does it come off?"

"It does. If I command it to do so."

"Fine. Drop the suit and I'll drop the gun. Probably couldn't get a shot off before you were on me anyway. I might look like a harmless old bitch, but I can and will put you on your ass if there's any funny business. Got it?"

I nod, then slowly slide my nail across my wrist, calling the inky black body armor to return. "As I stated before, I do not wish to harm you. I only wish to keep my Leigh safe."

Anya eyes me for a moment, the lines around her mouth pulling taut. "All right. But one false move and you'll regret it. I didn't survive this long trusting people, and I'm sure as hell not going to start with a big gray alien."

" I would expect nothing less. Now if we are finished, I would like to inquire about our current situation—"

Anya hits the button to restore the lights, and a loud static blares from the tiny box next to her. She holds up a hand. "Shh. Quiet. I've been waiting for this."

A male's voice begins to filter through a black machine on her desk. The majority of what is said is garbled and unclear.

"Damn it, I couldn't make it out. Could you understand it? They won't use that channel again, and it took me a week to predict which one they'd use next." She pauses for a second. "We've stopped trying to kill each other, right? Because this is really important."

I nod. These humans make no sense. Two seconds ago, she was hell bent on knocking me out and now she is asking me for help.

"Is it something that could assist in protecting my Leigh?" I ask, hesitant to gouge my own flesh if not necessary. The poison she infused me with has weakened my ability to heal. The language simulator in my brain records on a constant loop, and I can learn new languages through recall and replay. What was spoken will be recorded in there, but getting it out is going to hurt like hell.

"That's the ghost channel Elgin and his prick buddies use to speak to their government contacts. They rotate through them regularly. I've spent months trying to nail down the pattern, ever since Leigh told me she sunk Henrietta's predecessor, convinced he'd turn on her, and this was the first time I was right."

Needing no further explanation, I use my nail to dig into the back of my skull where my chip resides. The pain is not as significant as before when it required a reset. Anya pales when I come back with bloodied hands.

"Whoa, did you just cut that out of your brain?" she asks, face contorted in disbelief. Again, I do not understand her reaction.

"Do human males not sacrifice for their females?"

"Eh, they usually just take us out to dinner and even then, they expect to be praised."

Ah. No wonder they have evolved at such a slow rate.

After manually accessing its data bank, I replace the chip and utilize my abilities to reproduce the sounds.

"How'd you...you know what? It doesn't even matter." She grabs a writing utensil and places it on a thin white sheet. "Do it again, slower this time. Then I want to try something."

I indulge her, despite my desire to refuse. I do not see how this helps me or my Leigh, but the thoughtful set of her brow suggests she is close to finding whatever she needs to discern the human's next steps.

"Damn, the static covers it up no matter what we do." Anya sinks down in a chair and motions for me to do the same. "Sit over there, and don't worry. It's not booby trapped or nothing. If you want to prove you're not here to kill me and are really trying to protect our girl, here's your chance."

Our girl? I growl, letting my nails grow long enough to splinter the portion of the chair in my grip.

Anya throws up her hands. "Message received. She's yours. A little advice? Don't be telling her that. She's as independent as they come and wouldn't appreciate being labeled as property."

"Do not confuse my choice of words. Leigh is my *mate*. To cheapen that by assuming I would ever categorize her that way is a grave offense and one I do not take lightly." I stand and harden the set of my jaw.

"Slow down, cowboy. I was just makin' sure. I care about her, too, you know. Or else I wouldn't have risked my life to bring your ass here in the first place. If she didn't love you, I'd have left you to die in the woods."

Despite the crudeness of her words, I do not fail to see their value. "No one understands the need to survive more than me. I do not fault you for listening to your instincts."

Her wrinkled face scrunches up. "Really? I kind of expected more of a reaction. Some outrage, or I don't know, maybe another growl."

I nod, confused. In all the time I have spent with this female, I still cannot adequately analyze her reactions or interpret her next response. Humans are so complicated. I have no idea how they have continued to survive this long. Their facial expressions say one thing, and their mouths say another. Do these creatures ever say what they mean?

"Right. Let's get on with it then. See this right here? It is a private server that contains the video proof of your rescue and a log of all the communications between Elgin and the private contracting company he uses—transcripts, too. They have no idea, but he records everything. Little bonus to living on the island, you don't need two-party consent to be recorded.

"Problem is, I can't access it. It's protected with voice recognition software. Now, I hacked the program hiding it, and I know the password, but I can't copy a voice." Anya looks off into the distance at a set of numbers pinned to the wall and swallows hard. "If I could, I wouldn't be stuck here, hiding in plain sight, wishing I'd taken the blue pill.

"Anyway none of that is important. If you can clone this voice, I can destroy the proof he has of your existence and get you some of the information you need."

Rather than answer her, I repeat her words with her exact sound pattern. Explanations won't suffice for someone as untrusting as she is, but proof is undeniable. Plus, I've grown really fucking tired of this conversation. She's intolerable, and I miss my mate.

"Damn, that's...creepy as hell. Okay, let me pull up the recording. Hold on a minute."

Anya types furiously on her antique machine until she finds whatever she needs, then takes out a small black speaking device. The sound of a male's voice fills through the room, and it is one I will never forget.

A deep growl rumbles in my chest and I squeeze my hands into fists trying to curb my rage, and only the sweet scent of my mate and the patter of her feet on the floor soothe my demand for blood. She wraps her arms around me, and the mixture of our scents clinging to her skin make me want to rip off her clothes and take her again.

"Ugh, just hearing Elgin's voice makes me want to throw up. I remember that pompous, self-gratifying speech. It was at our pre-reveal of the Juniper wasn't it? Wait, you came? I begged you and you refused!"

"It was and I did. Just because I didn't announce it doesn't mean I wasn't there."

"You should have said something. I bitched at you for over a week for not coming."

"Why the hell are you out of bed? You need to sleep," Anya says, ignoring my mate's question.

Leigh twists the ends of my hair through her fingers. "I woke up to pee and he was gone. So, I came out here to make sure you weren't killing each other. Seems like things are going well."

The silver-haired female cocks a brow. "Yeah, better than I thought anyway. I figured by now he'd be on his ass passed out or I'd be dead. I never imagined this whole being civil thing."

"That's because you always assume people are out to get you," my mate says.

Scratching noises come from the room containing the furry overlord, and my mate glides over to open it. I love her curves and the way her hips move when she walks. By the ancients, I want to spend the rest of my existence exploring her.

As soon as she's free, the furry overlord scurries past my mate's open arms and begins curling around my ankles. Her scent clings to them as if she is trying to leave her mark. Ridiculous!

The creature called Bink howls obscenities when I pick her up by the scruff and hold her out to my Leigh, who then refuses her. And when the overlord begins to lament, I mimic her growl. She really is a wretched creature—leaving my mate to feel such negative emotions about her rejection.

"Every single time. I swear, as soon as he showed up on the boat, the little brat has snubbed me." My Leigh sniffles and jerks her chin toward me. The curve of her plump breasts swell when she crosses her arms to pout.

"That's new. You about to tell me he can talk to animals, too?"

My mate looks to me for permission to divulge the nature of my abilities. So loyal. It almost makes her lack of challenge over my being poisoned less bothersome. Perhaps she feels some ownership over me after all.

The furry overlord has jumped up on a nearby box, and after glaring at her, my mate pads over to slide into my lap. The feel of her round ass instantly hardens my cock, and my urge to take her is almost too much. After tasting her essence and feeling what it means to truly lose myself inside her, my need is insatiable.

"I can process and reproduce any audible language. Now, show me where you wish for me to speak and what you wish for me to say—" Arousal rises from the cleft between her thighs, and my mate arches her back, subtly grinding her sex against me. Sweet sky spirits, I'm about to lose control.

"Tread carefully, mate. Your friend has asked something of me, and I can only tame my need for you for so long," I whisper.

"Gross," Anya mutters, causing Leigh to laugh.

"Fine. I'll behave, I promise." After hopping off my lap, my mate grabs a nearby chair and sits. "All right, spy queen. What does he need to do?"

"Just clone Elgin's voice and say this sequence of numbers and letters into the mic."

"Right. Then we're drinking," Leigh says, slapping her hand on the table. "I've nearly died twice in the past day or so and I deserve to catch a buzz. Plus, it's not like we have anywhere to go right now anyway."

"No, booze. Not this time, Leigh. We need to be clear minded." Anya shakes her head and looks back at the two screens showing rotating camera views of the compound's exterior. No movement, and nothing appears to have activated the security measures she has put in place.

"Bullshit. You're drinking and we're going to have an honest conversation about what the hell all of this is," she gestures to the weapon-lined walls and the array of miscellaneous equipment, "because none of us even know if we're getting out of this alive."

A growl builds in my chest at the thought of losing her. "No one will take you from me."

"Simmer down. You know what I mean." Leigh hops up and starts opening cabinets and looking under the random piles of clutter lining the room until she finds a bottle of brown liquid and collapses back against her chair. "All right. You talk, then we all drink."

CHAPTER THIRTEEN

Leigh

Damn, he's so hot. Sitting here in a chair while Saxon does his voice thing with Anya, I can't take my eyes off of him. Sure our lives are in danger but fuck, he's everything I didn't even know I wanted in one gray, ripped package. And he's so sweet. You wouldn't think someone with razor sharp claws could touch you so gently.

Speaking of which, how in the hell does he make it feel so good when he puts them in my...you know what? I'm not going to question it. As long as he keeps it up, we're just going to call it what it is. A damn delicious miracle.

The awkward tension in the room has calmed. Either that or the four shots I just pounded made me care a little less. Saxon and Anya are both tense. They're cordial and working together to open the list of recordings she found of Elgin, but I can tell neither of them trust the other. Every word they say, every move they make is intentional. It's almost like watching a really fucked up game of chess where no one actually wins.

Hence my suggestion of drinking, but no one else wants to indulge. None of us have a freaking clue where to go from here. Saxon hasn't heard from his brother again, and I don't know how to explain it, but I know it hangs heavy in his mind. We don't know where his pod is or if it works. Elgin's still out there somewhere with his pay-as-you-go mercenaries looking for us. I'm sure the cops are too.

All because of my pride and determination. It's a really hard thing to admit. I sunk Henrietta. Sent years of work plummeting to the ocean floor and ruined my career. I was beyond devastated when I woke up, but I can't seem to muster the same emotion now.

Yes, I destroyed my entire life, but at the same time, I found Saxon, so I don't really know how to feel.

What if I hadn't screamed like a little girl and yanked on the controls? Or what if I'd let Elgin take the maiden dive and discover Saxon? Would my alien still want me like he does?

A chill skitters down my spine, and I wrap my arms around myself, cradling the bottle of booze like it's my only child. Elgin would never let Saxon see the light of day. He would die locked up somewhere or trying to escape, and neither of those situations is acceptable.

I just need to get him and his brother together, find his pod, and make sure I keep Anya safe in the process. Then I can spend a week processing the death of my life as I know it. Realization sits like a stone in my empty gut.

I don't know what's scarier. An alien showing up out of nowhere to claim me as his or the fact that I literally have no qualms about shoving my juicy ass into a little silver tube and jetting myself into the unknown to be with him.

Anya's computer dings, and I sit up taller to see what's going on. It's hard to decipher what's happening with her giant set-up. There's tech everywhere. And I thought my office back at the lab was a mess.

"We've done it. We're in, and that pesky little video of you two is gone. Now, we just need to upload your proof of Elgin's lies and we'll finally be getting somewhere." Anya grabs a set of headphones off the top of her desk. "I'm going to copy everything and move it to a separate drive so I can take my time and listen close. You two hang on. This is going to take a few minutes." She reaches over and snags the bottle out of my hand. "This is cause for a celebration. I might be able to keep you alive and out of Elgin's hands after all."

The bourbon drips down her chin as she throws it back and drinks right from the bottle.

Needing to feel him, I climb back into Saxon's lap. The slight buzz of the bourbon lowers my inhibitions, and right now the only place I want to be is wherever he is. Fitting since there really isn't anywhere else to go.

Like they were made for me, his hands mold to the curve of my hips, and damn, I love the way he touches me, "Hey," I whisper with a slight slur. The brightness of his eyes is so striking I have to swallow down all the cheesy stuff trying to pour out of me. "Thank you for helping Anya."

I run my nose along his jaw, enjoying his scent. We've been in the woods, in the sea and everywhere in between and he still smells clean. Like rain with only the slightest hint of sweat, it wraps around me and holds me just as tightly as his arms.

"I would pluck the very stars from the sky to keep you safe. If I understood the inner workings of this world, our enemies would already be dust. Your Anya is loyal and an invaluable resource. I would be a fool not to assist her when able."

"I love how you act like it's not a big deal. She nearly killed you once."

"Twice," Anya calls out, an edge of humor in her voice I haven't heard before. Seems bourbon affects her, too.

Saxon chuckles when my eyes widen and I ask, "What? When?"

He leans in close to whisper in my ear, and my nipples harden. "Before you woke, she attempted to challenge me."

"And you let her think she won, didn't you?" I lean inappropriately close. Saxon nods, and I press a kiss to his lips. It ends up being a little sloppier than I intended, but whatever. He doesn't seem to care.

When I pull back and look at him again, there's something not-so-little pressing against the seam of my ass. I love that I can affect him this way. It's empowering, and it might be the booze, but it makes me feel like the hottest woman in the world.

My stomach rumbles in a not so attractive way, and Saxon frowns. *"Mu Xitall..."*

"I'm fine. I'm not worried about eating right now. I want to hear what those sexy little slits on the side of your nose are for."

Anya swivels in her seat. "How long's it been since you ate? There's about a thousand calls logged in here, and they're taking forever to upload. If you two can manage not to procreate all over my floor, I'll go find the stash of MREs, dried fruit, and jerky I stuck somewhere in here last year."

Saxon lets out a little growl. "She's right, *Mu Xitall.* You need nutrients. Forgive me for failing to feed you. It will not happen again."

"Forgive you? Please. You've saved my life more times than I can count."

Before we can even finish our conversation, Anya's back and chucks a bag of dried apricots at my head. Saxon catches it before it collides with my face and stares at her, unamused.

She shrugs and clicks through the numerous camera views of the outside around the shelter and the edge of the tree line.

"All right, spy queen. Time to spill what and who the hell you are. How do you know how to do all this stuff?" I ask, mouth half full.

She gnaws on a piece of mystery meat then jerks her head toward Saxon. "Him first."

Oh, no. Anya does this kind of shit all the time. Answering my questions with some random demand that distracts me enough I forget what I asked in the first place. No way I'm letting her divert the conversation. Saxon opens his mouth answer, but I slap a hand over his mouth.

"He's from a planet named Revaris. Him, his brother, and a few other dudes who look like him hopped in a black hole to find their mates, had their travel ship thingy malfunction, got stuck under the ocean, and then woke to me nearly dying a few days ago.

"Happy? Now, stop skirting my question. Who are you, Anya?"

She crumples up the paper in her hands and rolls her eyes. "You know what I am. I already told you—wait! Did you just say he has a brother?"

Saxon stiffens at my side. "His name is Pavil. Why?"

Without warning, Anya pulls her legs off the table and launches herself toward the computer, spilling the jerky and nuts she was eating. "Shit. I think I've got something, and it's not good. I blew this off at first because I thought they were talking about you, but now I'm not so sure."

My stomach turns at the way she's furiously scrolling through the giant list of recordings. She's seriously going to leave it at that? "Anya, what is it? You're starting to freak me out. This better not be one of your lame-ass attempts to avoid answering questions."

Ignoring me completely, she slaps her headphones on one ear and looks at Saxon. "There have been sightings."

"Explain." His words are cold, and there's an edge of threat to them that I wasn't expecting. Suddenly, I feel a bit more protective of my friend.

"Damn it, I can't find it. I only played a few of the latest ones while the rest finished downloading so I wasn't really paying attention. But I could swear one in here mentions sightings all over the island of a gray monster freaking out the locals."

Saxon sighs. "Discreet has never been my brother's strong suit."

"Did they say anything else?" I ask.

"Hold on, I'm listening. I may have found the right one."

Saxon stands and begins pacing the room. "He will not allow himself to be captured. Many humans will die if they attempt to detain him. He has not found his mate. His instincts to survive will overpower him if he is cornered."

"Let's not go there yet, Saxon. We don't even know if that's really what she heard."

Anya holds up a finger. "It is. I've got it right here. It's from a few hours ago."

Shit. If that's the case, then Elgin's probably doubled his search efforts. My stomach sours at the thought of what would happen if Elgin got his hands on Saxon or his brother. Not to mention how many people would probably die.

"Is there any way to talk to him?"

Using one of his claws, Saxon peels back what looks like skin from his left wrist and starts messing with some sort of screen. "Not with a malfunctioning communicator. The only way I was able to contact Pavil before was when I was unconscious. As my brother, my soul calls to him when I am in danger. I have no other way to contact him now."

"I could dart you again," Anya offers.

"No!" Saxon and I answer in unison. "There has to be another way that doesn't leave him barely alive."

She throws her hands up. "Just a suggestion. You might want to figure it out quick, though, because according to this, they're going to search the area around the trench for Henrietta. They scanned the area and spotted something big enough to be her on sonar. As soon as the weather calms, they're going down."

If Elgin brings her up, he'll have all the proof he needs. Fuck. I'm such an idiot. I should have known not to make that internal recording.

"No. They can't have her. Elgin can't have proof."

"I already took care of that, I told you. I wiped the cloud. He doesn't have the video anymore," Anya says, exasperated.

"I made another one. I wasn't worried about it because I assumed the pressure of the trench would destroy the inside since Saxon ripped off the hatch, but if she's just on the ocean floor, there's a possibility the watertight storage compartments will hold. The chances are slim, but if the hard drive survived and those images of Saxon go public..."

Saxon's pacing increases and, without warning, he grabs the chair he was sitting in and crushes it in his hands. "Pavil will stay near his travel pod, wherever it is. He will not go far. And if he has located mine, he will protect it at all costs. I can find him."

Out of my chair before I can even think, I'm at his side. "No. You're not going out there. That's probably exactly what they want. How do we know this isn't a trap?"

"We do not. Leaving you is the last thing I wish to do, but what other choice do we have?"

For several seconds, the room's completely silent save for the sound of my heart in my ears. The smack of Anya tossing her notebook down startles me. "Fuck it, I'll go."

"Stop trying to be a hero, Anya. You've already done enough."

Heavy boots slap against the concrete after she yanks them on and once again dons her camo suit. Attaching a belt at her waist, she sticks more knives and guns in various holsters than I can count. "You asked me who I was, right? You wanted to know? Well, this is who I am. I was recruited out of the army into intelligence because I can hunt like a demon and kill soundlessly. I'm the best intelligence officer they ever had. I wanted out, they didn't agree, so I left, and they've been searching for me ever since.

"I've been doing this shit since before you were potty trained. I'll scout the beach and find out what they're up to and check all my normal resources for word on his brother. But you two need to figure out what the hell you're going to do and have a plan by the time I get back."

CHAPTER FOURTEEN

Leigh

As soon as the door slams behind Anya, my anxiety spikes a hundred notches. This feels wrong, and I need to do *something* to get my mind off of the chaos happening beyond these walls.

Her desk. There has to be a transmission or observation Anya's documented that can help us. While Saxon's using some of her tools to mess with the thing in his wrist, I start going through all of her notebooks but only find a mass of random data collection, people's movements and a whole lot of code words I can't understand.

There has to be a method to her madness, but I have no clue what it is. Saxon clears his throat, and I realize I've been clicking a pen non-stop to curb my anxiety. "Sorry, nervous habit."

He tucks his hair behind his ears and gives me a half-smile, then goes back to work after I set it down.

I scan the room for Binky only to find her cleaning herself. Well, there's a thought. I haven't showered in two days.

Between the sex and the clammy weather outside, I'm sure I smell like a real gem. Plus, with several layers of sweat and dirt clinging to me, my skin is itchy and uncomfortable.

Anya's desk squeaks when I push up to go search the back half of her place. Neither Saxon nor I have been seen it and with all the craziness, I hadn't even thought to look.

There are pipes running along the walls and ceiling in her command room, so I know she has to have a water pump in here somewhere. A purifier, I'd imagine, as well.

What in the actual hell is going on in here? As soon as I part the curtain she's using as a makeshift door, there are ammo boxes stacked to the ceiling, spare gun parts, lanterns, and what are these?–old beauty magazines?—haphazardly separated in piles. With every step, I learn something new about my friend. Who knew she was a *Cosmo* girl?

Nearly stumbling over a giant plastic tub of half created machines, I find a rudimentary shower.

My heart leaps at the thought of getting clean, and when I turn the dial and water begins to trickle out, I yank off my clothes with lightning speed.

The first few seconds are rough as my body adjusts to the coolness of the spray, but once I manage to relax, it feels like heaven. The scent of Ivory soap rises as I work the bar into the length of my hair and watch as streams of brown flow down the drain. Damn, I was dirtier than I thought.

A twinge of embarrassment warms my cheeks. I must have looked awful. Poor Saxon has never seen me anything but rough. I'm pretty sure the all-natural Leigh I've been rocking would have sent any normal human male running, life-threatening situation or not.

The air compressor in the tiny space kicks on, and the tolerance I've managed to build up to the cold water disappears, leaving my skin covered in goosebumps. I turn it off, not wanting to waste what little Anya probably has and just as I'm about to relent and force myself to get out, a familiar pair of hands wrap around my abdomen, instantly warming me.

Saxon. And he's very *very* naked.

"How'd you sneak in here like that?"

His lips are hot against my cool skin as he kisses my neck and tightens his hold. "Forgive my lack of consideration. Your beauty knows no bounds, *Mu Xitall*. The call of your body does things to me."

"Everything about you does things to me."

As he shifts his hips, his hard erection presses against my back, and I ache for him. Everything is so messed up. I just want to lose myself for a little. With one hand, I cup the back of his neck and stick out my ass, letting his cock nudge the seam of my entrance.

I want him there. No, I *need* him there, and I clench tight, unable to control my body's response to him. A deep growl builds at the base of his throat, and he guides me to the shower wall. He grips my thighs, spacing my feet further apart, then drops to his knees behind me.

My clit's throbbing, and in less than a minute, he's managed to turn me into a wild, needy mess. Pain sings across my skin when he bites my ass cheek, and the seam burns as he spreads me apart and dives in.

Knees trembling, I struggle to keep myself up. My hands slide against the slick shower wall, seeking support, but I find nothing. It's too much and not enough all at the same time and I feel like I'm about to burst.

The rooms spins, and a strangled yelp slips out as Saxon flips me around to face him. Without skipping a beat, he sucks my clit hard into his mouth, and the roughness of his teeth against my tender flesh has me crying out.

His muscles bulge underneath the small of my back as he

rises up and lifts me with him, guiding my thighs around his waist.

Without thought, I kiss him, letting my tongue dance against his—turned on even more now that he tastes like me.

"You are more exquisite than I could have imagined. More beautiful than I could have dreamed," he murmurs against my lips as he enters me. With nothing else to grab onto, I wrap my hands in his hair while he grips my ass and slides me up and down his length.

He holds me, thrusting in and out until I'm so jumbled up I can't figure out where he ends and I begin. We're all hot breath and whispered sweet nothings until he hits that special spot and I cry out, climaxing hard around his cock. He follows with his own release and then eases us both to the ground outside the shower.

My hair's tangled in my face, so I roll over onto my back and finger comb it into something manageable. When I lean back up on my elbow, I find him staring at me.

"What?" I ask, a hint of humor in my voice.

He reaches over to grab my hand and presses it to his lips. "Come with me."

"I kind of just did. Or didn't you notice all the screaming and clawing ..." I tug at his hands, expecting him to smile, but he doesn't.

"No, my Leigh. Come home with me. To Revaris. I know we have spoken of my desire to take you there, but I need to know you are ready. When we locate my pod, we may not have much time to prepare for our departure.

"I need to know you are with me not only here," he touches my forehead with the pad of his thumb, "but here as well." His hand covers my heart. "I am not blind to the sacrifices you will make. Our lives are in danger and we have little choice. But if we had met peacefully and did not have to endure such stressful circumstances, would you still desire to go with me?"

"Yes. I want to be wherever you are. Crazed maniac chasing us or not, I want to be with you, Saxon." The words tumble from my lips without thought, and I abandon his hands and scoot toward his open arms. He rests his head against mine and curls around me. I hold my breath, trying to decide how much to say. "I'm nervous. Before I met you, aliens were just probe-obsessed little green men. I know that's an ignorant thing to say, but it's the truth. The idea of jetting off into a giant vacuum in something half the size of a smart car terrifies me. But I love you, and the one thing that scares me more than the unknown is losing you."

Little zings of pleasure spread out across my body as he gently runs his claws down my back. "Probes? That is truly how your people see us?" he asks, smirking and I roll my eyes. "My people are not green and as you have seen first-hand, we are far from little."

"Trust me, I know. My body won't let me forget it."

A deep growl rattles his throat and he presses himself closer against me. "How am I to answer your questions when you tempt me in such a way?"

"In all fairness, I haven't actually asked you anything yet. But I would like to know what's going to happen once we get in your pod. Because we *will* make it out of here. You're not the only one who's waited their entire life to feel like this and I'm damn sure not going to let a tool like Elgin take it from me."

"Despite their size, our travel pods are designed to accommodate a mate with no issue. Once we enter, we are sedated and only wake once it is safe to exit. I would never put you in a position to be harmed. If I believed it unfit for travel, I would find another way to keep you safe."

Except, it already broke once didn't it? What's to say it won't do it again?

Shaking off the thoughts, I turn to explore his handsome face with my fingertips. "You don't know what's going to happen, do you?" My words are quiet, and I try hard to keep them free from judgement because I know none of this is his fault. I'll go either way, but for some reason I just need to hear him acknowledge it.

"I fear I cannot answer you completely, and it pains me to admit so. This process is romanticized amongst my people. Entering the black hole and coming back, mate in hand with stories of a fated meeting? That is our way, but our situation is different. Never before have I heard of an Exune facing what we have had to endure."

"Are you calling me *difficult?*"

I cock a brow, and he chuckles. "Our connection burns brighter than any I've seen, *Mu Xitall.* The threat of captivity and death are nothing in comparison to my fear of losing you. You encompass everything I have ever wanted and more, and I would carve out my own heart before I would allow you to be harmed."

"That's a bit extreme, don't you think? I don't think anyone is worth that amount of pain."

"I would do it. An existence without you is not worth living."

"Your heart is fine right where it is, no carving necessary," I say, patting his chest. Saxon grabs my hand and moves it lower. "Are you trying to put my hand on your dick in the middle of a life changing conversation?"

"My heart does not lie in my chest, *Mu Xitall,* but in my abdomen."

"Oh."

Well, that's embarrassing.

Saxon lifts my chin when I drop it and look away. "A creature as enchanting as you should never drop her gaze. You will find no judgement with me."

There is absolute truth to the way he says those words, and it leaves me devastated in the most romantic way. His devotion is heartbreaking and beautiful at the same time and it's through him I can find the courage to face the unknown without a solid plan.

For a total control freak, the idea of letting go is insane. But I love him, and everything else is just background music.

CHAPTER FIFTEEN

Saxon

"Breathe, *Mu Xitall*. I can feel your discomfort." Retracting my claws, I firmly massage the tight muscles of her neck while she leans over Anya's machines and stares at the security camera feeds. Ever since her friend left, with the exception of the few moments I managed to steal with her, she has focused solely on the hope of spotting the other female.

She seeks proof of life and carries a heavy guilt that her friend is now involved in our struggle. She has failed to remember that Anya inserted herself.

My Leigh leans back, resting her head on my shoulder. Her muscles have relaxed, but her mind still reels. "Ugh, why haven't we seen or heard from her yet? It's been like four hours."

"For a human, she moves in the shadows well. You are not meant to see her. I would be more concerned if we did."

She rubs her eyes, then grabs a few pieces of dried fruit Anya scattered across her desk earlier. "I hate this and I hate

Elgin. And after sitting here listening to these recordings, I hate myself for ignoring all the big ass red flags that were flying right in front of my face."

"I do not know these red flags you speak of, but just as you are not responsible for the valiant actions of your friend, you are not responsible for that piece of trash."

"No. I knew he was a selfish dick and I ignored it because I wanted to prove myself so badly nothing else mattered. I threw everything away—my family and friends—to work for a man I knew was unstable because no one else would hire me. He's a creep—a dangerous one—and if anything happens to you or Anya, I'll never forgive myself."

The loose strands of her yellow hair tangle in my claws when I brush them away from her face. The enticing curve of her lips calls to me as lean in closer, unable to maintain my distance. Even in the direst of times, my need for her knows no bounds.

"Thinking like that solves nothing. We must move forward. No matter the outcome, we have a course of action and a clear path. I know our meeting was abrupt and chaotic. You have suffered a great loss, been made to feel small and less than the magnanimous creature that you are, and I will not stand for it.

"This planet does not deserve you. The people here, save for your friend, do not deserve you. And I swear on everything I am that I will take you from this place no matter how many lives I must destroy in the process.

"My need for you and the strength of our connection cannot be contained by the laws of your people, nor the desires of the evil beings who seek to exploit us. Pavil lives. Our blood bond remains unaltered. He may be a cocky bastard incapable of common sense, but his machinery skills are unmatched and his loyalty unwavering. We will find him and then leave this spirit-forsaken planet."

My mate swallows hard, and my anger stirs at the pain and worry I see in her eyes. "What if we can't? I just don't know what I would do without you."

Her curvy body fits perfectly against mine when I wrap my arms around her. I despise her people for making her feel like this. This Elgin will pay dearly for the joy he has taken from her. "These humans feel they are invincible because I have allowed them to believe so. Rest assured, *Mu Xitall*. Anyone who stands in our way will pay."

A high pitched alarm sounds as the screen of Anya's computer lights up. Someone has tripped the perimeter sensors. *Movement detected in zones nine, fourteen, and twenty. Security breach! Security breach!*

Leigh jumps to her feet and stands before the blinking screens. "Anya? Is she back?" The hope in her voice drains as six males in black come into view. "Oh, shit. They've found us!"

They have not. The males continue to search the area but have not encroached beyond the perimeter. We are safe for now, but it is only a matter of time before they reach the entrance to our shelter.

"What do we do?" Leigh asks. Already short, her human claws are bloodied as she chews them to the quick. I grab her trembling hands and press a kiss to each, then guide her back to the safety of the room in which we slept.

I know what I have to do, and she is not going to like it. I cannot allow them to advance on our location without consequence. They will not get close enough hurt her.

War is the same no matter the universe, no matter the race. These vile creatures—these humans—know she is my weakness, and as any cutthroat soldier would, they exploit it. They will take her. Torture her. Leave her screaming until she begs for me and I answer.

The burn of outrage builds in my chest, flowing through my veins and lengthening my claws. No one will fucking touch her.

The hinges whine when I open the heavy door of the safe room to pull her inside. "Wait, what are you doing? We can't just sit here. What the fuck? We need to get out there and do something. Anya could come back and get ambushed!"

With a gentleness reserved only for her, I grab both sides of her face and claim her lips. I let her taste drive me, inspire me, remind me of what I am protecting, then as she begins to lean in and the scent of her arousal floods the room, I push her back and shut the door.

She is going to be so pissed, but that is preferable to dead or captured.

I cannot hear her words through the thick metal door, but her energy is wild and the scent of her outrage hangs heavy in the air.

I am going to pay for this for the rest of my existence. As long as she is there to complain, I am a luckier male for it.

Blocking my need to quell her distress, I slide my nail across my wrist and initiate my suit. A thrill of excitement builds in my chest, and almost as if my instincts were sentient, the need to hunt flares, and my mouth waters at the thought of their spilt blood.

Giving in to my baser side, I charge up the steps and stop at the entrance. The door is thick and reinforced but it cannot blunt my heightened senses. The humans remain far enough away that my exit should remain unseen. And if not, I will tear their tongues from their mouths so they cannot speak word of what they observed.

The air outside is sweet and carries with it eight separate scents. More have arrived. Splendid. The violence begging to be freed and consume my enemies will not be sated with their quick deaths. Perhaps a greater number will ease the itch to bask in their suffering.

The sound of their clumsy footsteps travels with the wind. I need to move quickly. My muscles burn as I charge at my full speed toward the largest group of scents. Earth's sun is low in the sky, letting the shadows of the trees hide me, and I watch, waiting for my prey to get in the perfect position.

These males continue to grunt and spew crass words as they fan out, using the inefficient light sources strapped to their weapons to illuminate the ground. Foolish pricks. Chests puffed out in confidence, they fear nothing. They do not even bother to watch for threats, believing themselves untouchable.

Lazily shuffling along, one male stops a few paces in front of me and kicks at the dirt. Voices begin to pour out of the communication device strapped to his shoulder. "You're looking a little butt hurt over there, Porzinga. Suck it up, bro."

"Hey, fuck off. I could be balls deep in my girl right now, but no, we're out here searching for a fuckin' gray ghost and some lab bitch who pissed off the wrong rich tool." He continues several steps then squats to haphazardly search through a pile of brush with the butt end of his weapon. "This is a waste of fuckin' time. There isn't anything out here."

The communicator goes off again. "Stop whining and do your job. That rich tool offered us half a mil to find that so-called lab bitch. Get your head out of your ass and look."

"You know, I gotta wonder about that. What's this girl got? A golden pussy or something? She must give one hell of a blow—"

As soon as the filth he speaks translates, all rational thought stops. Red. All I see is red, and the smell of blood saturates my pores. Flesh wedges itself underneath my claws and I'm showered in gore as I rip out his throat, as if removing his head will remove the stain of his vile words.

By the time my vision returns, he's nothing more than a pile of slop at my feet. What a fucking mess.

"Porzinga? Where you at, asshole?"

Grabbing the communicator I swipe off the filth and respond. "Takin' a piss. I'll see you fucks soon."

And I will. With pleasure.

Returning to the shadows the setting sun provides, I speed with precision toward where the other males have clustered. Slowly, they have moved closer to my mate. And when I see they have split into two groups of three with one lingering behind, I know what I need to do.

Faster than the human eye can detect, I yank the straggler off his feet by the neck, severing his spine, and then run back into the trees to impale him on a high hanging branch where is he mostly out of sight.

The male leading the first group turns, shining his light on the spot where his soldier once stood. "Where the fuck did Frazier go?" he asks, annoyance and concern infusing his tone. I do not give the rest enough time to answer.

Letting my instincts roar to life, I summon my energy shield and plunge myself into the middle of their formation and attack from all sides. I start with the throats, imperative to silence their screams, then slice at each major organ until I can see their insides on the ground and do not stop until they lie crumpled beneath me.

As the last heart ceases to beat, the violence-induced rage commanding my mind eases, and I claw at the ground, removing large armfuls of earth to bury the evidence of their deaths and restore some respect to those who created them.

I do not care to take life unless it is necessary, but there are parts of me that delight in the scent of fresh blood.

Using the last of my shield reserves, I focus on the remains and burn them, destroying any possible equipment that could signal their location.

Sweat drips from my brow—my own hands torn from my efforts—and gore clings to my suit. Inhaling once more to check for additional scents, one in particular reaches my nose.

Anya. She bleeds. And she is closer than I expected.

She will have seen the entire massacre first hand. Unsure of her tolerance, I approach slowly, ensuring my steps are loud.

"A little help, please?" Her voice is weary and does not contain the normal amount of defiance. She is exhausted and hurt, shielding herself from sight by hiding up in a tree. "I've been stuck here for two hours trying to avoid those dickheads. They started at the beach and worked their way here looking for you and Leigh. I thought I lost them, but when I reached the tree line, I saw their Jeeps and realized they were headed here."

"You are wounded?" I ask, catching her. She grimaces at the mixture of human and Revari blood that transfers to her own clothing, then cradles her ankle in her hand as soon as she sits on the ground.

"Dislocated it trying to hop over a fallen tree. I'm too old for this shit, man. You're obviously on your game. I mean damn, what you just did out there was something out of nightmares. It made me cringe, and I've done some really messed up stuff."

"I hold no mercy for those that threaten me and mine."

"Right. Where is she, by the way? Surely, you didn't bring her out here."

"I locked her inside the shelter."

Anya does the most unexpected thing. She bursts in to laughter amidst her pain. "Oh, lawd, have mercy. She's going to kick your ass, you know that?"

"I am aware." Judging by the pure rage she felt when I left, I am going to be paying for this for a while.

As if it is commonplace, she grabs a discarded tree branch and clenches it between her teeth, then holds up her swollen ankle. "Help me out, eh? I can't walk on the son of a bitch, and I'm not too keen on being carried. We need to get back. What I found at the beach wasn't good."

Leigh

Motherfucker. I'm going to kill him. No, I'm going to punch him in the balls. I can't believe he did this to me. Locking me in here while he goes out there to get himself killed?

What the hell? There are exactly four people in this world I care about, and one of them isn't even a damn person. My sister hates me, Anya's missing, and now Saxon rushes into danger and leaves me locked in here?

Fuck. What if they never come back?

A sudden bout of nausea twists my gut, and I lean over to retch. The few pieces of dried fruit I ate come right up, and the walls start to close in. I've never been claustrophobic but the idea of being trapped all alone? And knowing Binky is stuck in here too, wondering why I abandoned her while she runs around scared and hungry?

I need to get out. Right fucking now.

The pressure in my head nearly sends me to my knees, and my heart's racing. Hysteria is taking over, and no matter how many times I tell myself to calm down, it does nothing.

I can't breathe. I can't think about anything other than getting out.

With trembling fingers, I key in Anya's code to open the door. But it doesn't work. So, of course I try again. And again. And again. Saxon must have overridden it, and I know it's useless, but I can't keep myself from pounding on the buttons.

Then on the door. Screaming for him to let me out, over and over until my voice is hoarse.

I lost my chance at having a relationship with my sister and my niece. I've come to terms with that. It's an ugly truth but it's one I can swallow. But Anya? She's risked her life for me time and time again, and I can't do anything to help her. I've spent my entire adulthood ignoring the needs of others in favor of my own selfish desires, and now that I'm faced with the chance to change and make a difference, I can't.

I always thought I'd be better off alone and people will only disappoint and betray me, and now the two people I care most about in the world are out there and quite possibly dying and I can't do shit to help them.

If I lose either one of them, I won't be able to forgive him. Or myself.

Like overinflated balloons, my lungs feel like they're about to explode. My vision tilts, and I sag to the floor with my head between my knees trying to block everything else out and just breathe.

I can't lose them. I don't care about my career or my reputation or even myself. Just please...let them both come back alive.

My heart leaps into my throat at the sound of the locks disengaging, and I blink hard trying to clear my vision. The sight of Saxon's claws wrapping around the edge of the door inspires pure joy as well as a healthy dose of pre-pubescent teenage girl rage.

Not caring about how ridiculous I look, I launch myself at him and wrap my arms around his waist. As soon as he reciprocates the embrace, I shove him back, hard.

"You asshole! I can't believe you did that to me!" I yell, pounding my fists against him again.

He holds up his hands. *"Mu Xitall—"*

"No! Don't *Mu Xitall* me, you big scary bastard! That was not okay!" The burst of outrage that inspired my courage dies like a flame in the wind, and I'm left with nothing but raging emotion. Tears sting my eyes, and when I push him this time, it's half-hearted. "You left me in there. I was so worried about you. What if you didn't come back for me, huh? I would have been stuck in there mourning you until I died alone!"

Chest heaving, I sag into his arms when he holds me once again, not even caring that he's covered in absolute filth. He's alive.

"Oh, calm your tits, Leigh. There's no way he wasn't coming back for you. Guy's a fucking killing machine. There were guts flying everywhere."

Anya!

Nearly falling over from the quick transition, I fling myself at her, and she yelps, then we both fall to the floor. "Easy. My ankle is jacked up. Your boy here had to reset it right after he slaughtered all those poor bastards searching for you. Whatever he did worked because damn, I can actually move it now."

"What took you so long? You scared the shit out of me. Five hours, Anya! Really? You have so many gadgets here and you didn't think to take a fucking walkie talkie or something so we'd know if you were still alive? I was worried sick!"

After wrapping her in another embrace, I scoot back on the floor and glare at them both. I'm so very happy they're alive but damn, if I'm not angry at them both. I know it's ridiculous. I knew Anya was leaving and that we didn't have another choice, but I can't control my reaction. My people are alive. That's all that matters. Plus, he locked me in a room. I have a full license to be a bitch.

"Yeah, well between Elgin's minions and the government guys setting up tents on the beach, I had a hard time staying hidden. Hey, where the fuck is my number? The number pinned right up there?"

She jumps up and starts frantically searching for it.

When I grab it off the desk where I set it, she clutches it in her hands and exhales. "Don't ever fucking touch this. It's the key to everything."

Saxon tenses, and I nearly cough on my spit. "Okay, sorry. I won't. Geeze. Now if you're done being a spaz queen, tell me about these tents."

"They found something and are keeping it locked up tight."

"My travel pod."

A sense of dread washes over the room. Saxon's stoic, and I can only imagine all the things running through his mind. He hates it here. Loves me, but after hearing how passionate he is about taking me to his home, I can imagine how devastating it might be to learn it will be impossible.

We can't let Elgin have Saxon's travel pod. It represents so much more than just a ship. It's the death of his dreams and if the general public or the government gets ahold of something that proves aliens do exist, the entire planet will be searching for him. That's no way to live.

Fuck this. No one's going to take this from him. Or me.

I guess I wanted to go more than I even realized.

"We're going to get it," I say, pulling myself up by the edge of her desk.

Anya shakes her head and points to her ankle. "You see this? They forced me into a tree for four hours. You really think you and a big ass gray alien can go in there unseen and sneak it out? You're insane. Not happening."

"We don't have another choice." I'm not budging. I have no freaking clue what we're going to do, but all Saxon's wanted since the second he woke up and saved my life was to love me and take me home to meet his people. He doesn't deserve to be threatened or hunted for the personal glory of some rich prick with short man syndrome.

He's a good man—a strong man—and he's mine. It's about time I started acting like it.

"So, think of another one. What you're talking about is suicide, Leigh. There must be fifty people crawling all over that tiny part of the beach, and they've got people on security. You won't make it ten feet before someone sees you."

She jerks her thumb toward Saxon, who's still pacing and fiddling with whatever is embedded in his wrist. "If you blow through there like hell on wheels, the collateral damage will be insane. There are a ton of people out there who don't deserve to die just for being on Elgin's dime. They aren't soldiers. Not all of them anyway."

"I have never killed an innocent and do not intend to start now."

My throat tightens at the hard set of Saxon's jaw and the emotion swirling in his eyes. He's still a mess and his hair is wild but nothing stands out more than the pained expression on his face. Whatever conclusion he's come to distresses him, and I know what he's going to say before the words even come out of his mouth. It's the thing he's avoided thus far, and now he doesn't have a choice.

"No."

"You were right, *Mu Xitall*. We have no other choice."

"I'm not doing this shit again. You're not leaving me here to wonder what's happening to you. Or if you're safe. I can't—" my voice wavers, and no matter how hard I try to steady my lip, it trembles anyway.

"I can no longer rely on Pavil. I need to wake the others. Together we can safely take back what belongs to us."

Anya waves her hands in the air. "Hello? Anyone paying attention? I just told you the beach is crawling with people searching for you. What the fuck are you planning to do, space man? Swim all the way out to the trench and dive down yourself?"

Saxon stops pacing and meets my gaze. That's exactly what he's planning.

I don't exactly like the idea, but it's not the worst I've ever heard. I know Saxon can handle the pressure because he survived once before. And that far down, no one else could touch him, especially if Henrietta is out of commission.

"It could work," I muse with a shrug. "And I could hide somewhere in the shallow part of the water off-shore to make sure they don't decide to drag the ocean floor for Henrietta while he's out there."

"You will not come." Saxon crosses his arms and straightens as if that's enough to shut me up. Please. There's no way in hell I'm letting him order me to stay. And fuck following him into that stupid room again.

"Are you two serious right now? Neither of you are going. It's the dumbest fucking plan I've ever heard. You might as well walk right up to Elgin, bend over, and let him shove that silver spoon of his right up your ass."

Narrowing my eyes at Anya, I jut out my jaw trying to exude the confidence I don't feel. "It'll work, I'm going, and I don't want to hear another single thing about it."

CHAPTER SIXTEEN

Leigh

"You're going to need a lot more than hope to make this happen," Anya says, tossing me a 9mm gun. It's heavy and cold, and I have no idea how to use it. It feels so wrong to leave Binky and Anya behind to go with Saxon. But it feels even worse to leave *him*, so I don't know what to do. "Real life isn't like the movies. Don't get it wet; it won't fire for shit. And if you point it at someone, be ready for them to die, because otherwise you'll miss and end up on the wrong end of it."

She pulls at the harness she's strapped on me like a backpack, making sure it's tight, then takes another gun off her table and slides it into the holster.

"Thank you for this."

"It's suicide, and I refuse to be a part of it. It also pisses me off that I've exposed myself to save your life and you're just going to piss it away by doing something fucking stupid. But I get it. I know I can't change your mind. At least, this way I know you have the tools you need."

"Saxon's the one doing all the work. I'm just going to sit by and be ready to create a distraction if they approach him. If no one comes, I'll stay hidden the entire time."

Anya laughs in a sad sort of way and straightens the wrinkled part of my shirt. "You're impossible not to notice, friend. Even for a crazy bitch like me."

There's a finality to the way she's looking at me. Almost as if she thinks it's going to be the last time. "Why do I feel like you're saying goodbye?"

"Because even though I love you, Leigh. I can't get behind this insanity. At some point, I've got to protect myself and prepare for the worst. If you don't come back, I'll still be stuck. When you leave with him, I'll still be forced into the shadows and eating cold food for the rest of my life, and nothing's ever going to change that. If we've got to say goodbye, now's as good a time as any."

The room starts to feel too hot as tears burn my eyes. "That was...fucking harsh."

"I know. And I don't mean for it to be. But it is what it is."

I nod, trying to swallow the lump in my throat and find something to say but I can't. I guess I didn't really realize up until this moment how much she really means to me. I've been so wrapped up in what it would be like to jump into the unknown with Saxon, I didn't really think about how it would feel to leave her behind.

Or Binky.

Heavy tears slide down my face and I do my best to collect myself. Can I really do this? Leave the two friends who have stood by me for most of my adult life?

Anya smiles and leans back on her desk. "It's Sue, by the way. Not Anya. I only used that name because she was my favorite character on *Buffy*."

Her honesty warms me, taking away a bit of the misery settling in my chest and I laugh. "Bitch got such a bad rap. I can't see myself calling you anything else."

"Ha! She did, and it's all good. I've been someone else for so long I don't remember what it's like to be Sue anyway," Anya mutters.

Almost as if she can sense the tension, Binky jumps up on the table near us and paws at me to pick her up. "You don't have to do this, you know? No offense, but you're basically going out there for nothing. You can't do shit. With as far away as Saxon's planning to be, anyone on the beach won't hear you anyway."

"I have to try."

As always, Binky begins to purr when I hold her close, and the vibration settles me. She might be a diva—a slightly promiscuous one, apparently—but she's been my counselor, my friend, and my nighttime snuggle companion during the worst and best of my life here on the island. This is the hardest decision I've ever had to make.

It might sound dumb because she's only a cat, but it's going to kill me to leave her.

"I hate that you have to live like this. I didn't realize it was this bad," I say, giving my furry friend one more hug. Anya swipes her hand through the air in a dismissive way and grabs Binky out of my arms.

"Enough, girl. This shit isn't going to get any easier and you're wasting time. You need to stop worrying about me and focus on keeping yourself alive."

I nod, then pull Anya and Binky into one last hug.

Her voice trembles when she says, "If you leave, you can't come back here."

"I know." As I pull away, I can't resist the urge to nuzzle

Binky's head once more. Fuck, I love this stupid cat. This is so hard. I feel like my heart is ripping in two.

Saxon wraps an arm around my shoulders and presses a kiss to the side of my face. "Stay, *Mu Xitall.*" His eyes search mine. "You mourn your separation from the furry overlord and your friend. There is no need to choose between us. I will travel faster and be less distracted without you." He clenches his teeth and looks to Anya. "It is safer if you remain here."

His words bounce off the surface of my mind but they don't sink in. It's almost like I can't comprehend them. "You're asking me to let you go without knowing if I'll ever see you again? That's not some shit you get to decide by yourself."

Saxon shakes his head. " Stop being so stubborn and listen to me. I am asking you to trust me. Stay with Anya. She will keep you safe. It is the best way." He slides his claw across his wrist in the shape of a crescent moon identical to the mark we both wear and grabs my hand. Rather than cover him completely, the tiny black scales of his suit climb up my arm and wrap around my shoulders and chest.

The remaining part of his suit spreads across his skin, but the thickness over his own upper body is noticeably thinner.

"No, take it back. You need it. This isn't what I meant."

"Well, it is what you get. I need to know you are safe. This is the only way to ensure that." He drags a claw across the suit on his belly roughly, and the scales that cover my chest vibrate. "We can feel each other—know if the other is in pain. If you fear for your life at any time, mark your suit and I will come for you."

"Swear? Because if you die, I'm going to be so pissed."

Saxon kisses me hard then yanks open Anya's shelter door. "By the ancient sky spirits, *Mu Xitall.* I will give you the world I promised you and no one will stand in my way."

Saxon

Every single part of my being screams for me to return to her. To lash out at any living thing with breath that comes near and chew and claw my way back home.

Leaving her in the care of another goes against all that I am but I cannot take her with me. It is a selfish thing, to want her always by my side, and foolish to assume I can enter the wet ooze and keep her safe.

If the ancient sky spirits meant for her to go with me, they would have made her body able to withstand the harsh conditions of the liquid prison.

I wish that I were a creature of pure violence. That like many other breeds, could tolerate the useless bloodshed conquering a planet calls for. I would simply give in to my instincts and hunt until there was no one left to challenge me. I have the skill and fortitude to do it.

After witnessing such violence, my people chose another way. They decided to honor life and charged those of us expected to find our mates in another world to uphold those expectations and kill only when necessary.

With my brethren at my side, I can obtain what is mine without dishonoring myself and those who created me. If the humans still foolishly resist and seek to harm us, then we will annihilate them more efficiently.

No matter how the ancient sky spirits have destined this to play out, I have gone above and beyond to please them. My bond with Leigh will be blessed, and this wretched place can be left to consume itself.

After clearing the beach and diving beneath its unforgiving

surface, the wet ooze saturates my senses, blanketing and stealing away the scent of my mate. A pleasant warmth—so uniquely her—has lingered since the moment I first felt her flush against my skin and now it's gone. I miss it. And I miss her. I did not anticipate reacting this strongly to her absence and the strength of my emotions catches me off guard.

This planet fucking sucks. Without her scent to distract me I am left with nothing but my own thoughts. This spirit-forsaken liquid creeps into every pore as I push harder and faster, opening my every sense to listen and observe. I have to get to Cyfer and Ajax.

To a Revari male, failing to return home is seen as the ultimate disappointment. Those who do not are mourned as if they are dead. An image of them is constructed from tizi buds and burned to ash, a symbol of returning us to the skies.

If I fail, my mother and father will spend two moon rises without sustenance, bringing themselves as close to our spiritual existence as possible to say their final goodbyes. They will lament the loss of not one but two progeny and the two females we would have brought into our collective.

It will leave them devastated, and they are too old to rebreed. My mother will never receive an honor ceremony where her fertility is celebrated as the spark that started the fire of life my mate and I will carry on. I will not damn them to an existence without the laughter of Revari babes at their feet.

Screw that.

Unlike the Earthen beasts that roam on four legs, those that dwell inside the wet ooze are unconcerned with my presence. Even the largest greets me with ease. His deep crooning call welcomes me, warning me of the sharp-toothed predators who also call the wet ooze their home.

My hands ache for violence—any outlet to release the frustration and anger setting me on edge. Where the fuck is Pavil?

Has he done any of the things I have requested of him? Or has he found his mate somewhere and completely ignored my call to arms?

He better have a damn good explanation for why I had to swim down here to wake the others. Surely, even at his most distracted, he would not fail to comprehend the gravity of the situation we have landed in. Frivolity has always called to him more than a traditional male, but he too feels the unmovable drive to fulfill the call of the Exune.

Now is not the time to lose my faith in him. Or the ancient sky spirits. Even they would not have given me a taste of what an existence with a being as unimaginable as my mate is like only to take it away.

I will consume the universe if she was taken from me.

Almost as if pushing myself harder can drive the thoughts from my mind, I punish my muscles, embracing the burn. The atmosphere on Revaris, like Earth, offers high concentrations of oxygen.

The stark decrease of its availability down this low begins to strain my body, and using my secondary passages to break down and absorb the dissolved oxygen requires almost the amount of energy it yields.

I cannot sustain this level of exertion for long, but fuck if I do not want to get back to my mate as quickly as possible. Forcing myself to slow, I glide through the wet ooze, giving my eyes time to adjust. It is much easier than it was when I first awoke to Leigh's call.

The complete blackness of the wet ooze allowed for no light, and it was only through the self-emitting light of the surrounding creatures and the tiny amount that came from my communicator that I was able to visualize my surroundings.

Swimming the remainder of my journey at the extreme

depths I experienced before is not an option. I am not even halfway there and am already fatigued.

It is not until I decrease the angle of my descent and rise a fraction, that I notice the call of a collective of the ooze beasts I heard before.

They sing of their devotion to each other. And their love of the wet ooze and its gracious offering of food. I beg to differ. This place is pure misery, but the beauty of their song makes it almost bearable.

I pause to absorb the melody, committing it to memory. It is a risk, but my female has a fondness for these types of sounds, and it is customary to offer a mating gift on our arrival. With our complicated relationship, I have not had time to prepare. The chance to surprise her in such a way outweighs the loss of time and energy it requires.

The song travels through the wet ooze beautifully and, as it comes to an end, the largest beast's song is interrupted by the scream of its youngling. It claws at my sensibilities, demanding I respond, and as I surge forward to find the source of its pain, a wall of energy consumes me.

Contorting with each wave of energy released, I fight to stay conscious. A machine whirls above as I float nearer to the surface, and the craft flying overhead casts a shadow, blunting the light beginning to trickle in. Death surrounds me. One tiny beast after another takes its last breath as repeated bursts of electricity course through the water.

These innocent creatures do not deserve to die. All of this useless suffering to obtain me? At what cost?

With pain and outrage as fuel, I force myself to endure and swim closer to the source. I could escape. The current they are using is not strong enough to leave me incapacitated, only weak. But to allow this to continue will be a stain on my soul I could not wash off.

What is strength for if not to protect those who cannot protect themselves?

I force myself into the center of the current. Slowly tearing its way through my body, the impulse burns me from the inside out until I've reached the tip of the spirit-forsaken device delivering it.

Air bursts from my lungs, and I roar as I wrap my arms around the giant barb and squeeze. The metal crunches and bends until the devastating impulses stop. The few creatures still able swim away do so, and with the last of my energy, I climb the broken death spike, using my claws to steady me.

These murdering assholes cannot be allowed to live. The wails of the creatures mourning their loved ones spur me on, and once I reach the surface of the water, I can see nothing but the fucks responsible for so much pain.

Their voices carry. "Get him off! Get him off! He's going to take us down." Panic, fear-induced yelling snakes through the sound of the craft's blades spinning, and even through the spray of the sea in the air I can scent their fear.

Good. It is their turn to be afraid.

Alarms ring out as the male pilot jerks to the right, attempting to shake me off, but I hold tight and crawl my way up, snagging a hand on the landing gear. Releasing himself from a belted chair near the open door, the first male pulls a small black weapon.

Too little too late. He screams as I snap both his legs and throw him to the wet ooze below. He will suffer slowly, seeing the life he stole as he takes his last breaths. The second male attempts to pull his own weapon, but I crush his fist and rip him from the seat by his neck.

The alarms scream as the craft hurtles toward the water, and because those who suffered deserve to receive their vengeance in kind, I tie the male with the binds meant for me and secure him to the chair. He will also die a watery death as so many others have today.

As the craft plunges beneath the surface, the last fiber of my strength fades, and I succumb to my bodies demand to heal. I failed in waking the others and I only hope my mate can forgive me.

CHAPTER SEVENTEEN

Fifteen minutes earlier...

Leigh

I'm going to vomit or nervous poop or something in between and it's been like this since Saxon disappeared into the trees. Worrying about him is making me physically ill. No wonder I didn't sign up for this relationship stress in my twenties. Caring about someone other than yourself is fucking hard.

"Here's another one. Holy crap, Leigh. Sterling's trying to get the FBI involved in all this mess. Why in the hell didn't you say something before?" Anya asks after listening to another one of Elgin's messages. This time it was between him and the CEO of Daxx Corp discussing how much I stole and how Elgin just so happened to have a boat load of evidence that magically fell into his lap.

"I don't like conflict. I knew he was a megalomaniac but I

thought all the money stuff was just part of me keeping my job. You know, punishment for my initial failure."

She narrows her eyes. "You should have squashed this weeks ago. If all of this hadn't been drudged up, you'd have been able to ride into the sunset with alien boy and avoid all this drama."

Grabbing the tennis ball I've been bouncing against the wall for the past twenty minutes, I throw it as hard as I can right at her head.

She catches it without even looking and it pisses me off even more. "Can we focus on what to do and not what I should have done, please? I already feel bad enough Saxon's out there by himself, I don't need your judgmental ass throwing salt in the wound."

"Someone had to say it, and I don't see anyone else around, do you? Binky can't talk, but I can guarantee if she could, she'd have chewed you a new one."

Just the mention of her name makes me smile. She's such a brat, but I love her and after feeling how I did about leaving her earlier I know now I never could. I don't care if I have to smuggle her in my cleavage, my fur ball is coming with me. "Where is the little harlot, anyway? It's past time for her to eat."

Anya stops typing and turns to look at me. "Binky? Missing a meal? When's the last time you actually saw her?"

With all the craziness of the emotional whirlwind I've been through, I can't actually recall. But she has to be here, right? Binky never leaves my side. Unless...

My lungs deflate, and a feeling of pure horror overtakes me. "Right before Saxon left."

"You don't think she'd follow after him do you?" Anya asks, already out of her seat on her way to the stairs.

Shit. "Binky!" I call out, running around the command room like a crazed lunatic. She's not in the back or where Anya sleeps. The safe room is closed...she did it. She ran after him. I just know it.

Heart in my throat, I take the stairs three at a time, knocking Anya out of the way.

"Hey, wait a second, Leigh. Calm down. We'll find her. Let me just check the cameras and turn off the perimeter alarms and then I'll help you—no stop!" she yells but it's too late. I've already unlocked the massive shelter door and thrown it open.

My throat's dry, and I can't get enough air as I cup my hands and start calling Binky's name. The sun is bright in the sky, and it burns my eyes after being underground for so long. I can't find her anywhere so I head for the tree line. She wouldn't have gone in the water no matter how badly she wanted to follow him. She has to be somewhere between here and there and, damn it, I'm going to find her.

Running in a blind panic, I call out for her and search everywhere I can think, and by the time my wits kick in and I realize what I've done, I'm already at the edge of the beach Anya spied on earlier today.

Jumping behind a nearby boulder, I try to keep myself hidden. All of Elgin's people are more than two miles down the sand, but I can't take a chance on them seeing me. Any more than they already did since I went running toward them like a total dumb ass.

I have got to work on my life choices.

Glancing around the rock again, I scan the beach to get a better look. It doesn't seem like it's just Elgin's guys there. There's an unmarked government Jeep parked close to the road and a big shipping container set up next to a bunch of white canvas tents.

I squint, trying to make out what else is behind them. Some type of hydraulic crane, but the other shape looks like...

A prison transport truck? Wait, what would Elgin need

that for? From what I saw of Saxon's travel pod, it won't fit in there. Plus, even if it could, wouldn't a different kind of armored car be better?

I mean, those trucks are only good when you're going to be transferring—*oh, shit.*

A sick feeling swamps me, and I swallow hard as my brain fights to come up with another reason for it being there.

There isn't one.

Swinging around, I scan the horizon looking for a ship or a boat, something that Elgin would use to trap Saxon, but I can't see anything that far out.

Have they found Pavil? Are they keeping the truck there just in case he shows up? Or is it for me? What are they planning?

Paranoia sets in, and I double checking my surroundings. I don't see anything out of sorts, and there's nothing but the sound of waves pounding against the beach.

"Leigh, get over here now!" Anya whisper-yells while waving me back toward the tree line. "What are you trying to do? Get yourself killed?"

After giving the beach one more look, I push off the boulder and scurry back to her. Something's wrong. I can feel it in my gut, and Binky's still nowhere to be found.

Anya clinches her teeth like she's about to smack me then takes a deep breath. "You can't just run out of there like that. It's stupid and inconsiderate. Someone could have seen. There are smarter ways to do this."

"I'm sorry! I panicked. I'm not like you. I can't just be all robotic and shit when the people and things I love could be hurt. Why are you out here anyway?"

"Oh, you know. Just taking a nice stroll—I'm out here because I'm trying to keep you alive, something you refuse to do. Another transmission popped up on Elgin's server right before you decided to lose your mind. They dispatched something called an EEL. Which I could have told you if you had of just waited five damn minutes for me to check everything."

EEL. EEL... Why does that sound familiar?

A memory of a conversation I had with Elgin flits through my mind. I rarely listen to him, so it's hard to fully recall, but warning bells are going off in my head, and I can't remember why.

Think, Leigh. Think.

I rub my hands on my thighs and start to pace. It was right after Christmas and he was bragging about something he'd managed to get the patent for, but I thought it was stupid. It had to do with fishing, which was ridiculous, because that's a primary source of local income here and creating a machine that would put people out of a job would be a total dick move.

Time slows as the image of the designs he showed me burst to life in my mind. An electric probe delivered via helicopter that lowered into the water and stunned the fish long enough for an industrialized strength net carried on board to deploy and swoop them up.

But I don't understand. The committee wouldn't approve it because the voltage was too high. It wasn't safe...

Fuck. It's a trap. He must have built it anyway and they're going after Saxon.

An animalistic wail pours out of me as I lunge for the beach, and Anya tackles me to the ground. "What the fuck is wrong with you? Talk to me, Leigh!"

"It's a probe. They're going to...electrocute...him...in the water," I manage as I struggle to get free. Anya's way stronger than I am, but when a wave of pain greater than I've ever felt radiates across my chest, I can't breathe.

Veins bulging, I arch my back—my vision going white. I can hear Anya's voice telling me to shut up and not to scream and I can feel her shaking me but I can't speak. As soon as the pain subsides, Anya's panicked face comes into view.

"Hold tight. Tell them nothing. I'll come back when the time's right."

Wait, what? Where's she going? Is she seriously leaving me right now?

The dirt bites into my elbow as I push myself up and look around. Anya's gone and the familiar scent of cologne tickles my nose.

"Hey, Leigh."

I jerk to my left, losing my balance and nearly face planting on the ground. "Joseph?"

"I'm really sorry about this, Doc. I wouldn't if I had another choice."

"Whatever you're about to do, don't. Let's just talk about this—" Agony explodes across my scalp as Joseph smashes me in the head with the butt of his gun. As my world fades to black, the last thing I feel is Joseph lifting me in his arms.

CHAPTER EIGHTEEN

Saxon

My mate's breasts are firm beneath my grip and the tiny mounds that grace their middle harden under my touch. "Saxon," she mewls, reaching down to grab my cock. She guides it toward her entrance, thrusting her hips, begging for it.

"More," she demands, rubbing the wet warmth of her folds against the tip of my cock. "I want you inside me, use all of your brute strength to—"

"Brute strength, brother? Really?" The pleasantry of my mate's warmth is ripped away by the sound of Pavil's voice and the lingering pain of my injuries charges into my awareness. Fuck, that was a great dream, and I am annoyed he interrupted it.

"You need to wake, brother. Wherever you are, I can feel you fighting to survive."

Alive, but still floating somewhere on the surface of the wet ooze, I can hear vibrations in the water. The humans are coming for me.

"Fuck off. Where have you been? I was attacked trying to do the thing I asked you to do more than a star rise ago."

"How many times is this now? These humans are on a roll."

"Do you take nothing seriously? This is not the time to screw around, Pavil. Our return to Revaris and my mate bond are at risk. These humans are morons. I received word they have my pod. There is no telling what they will screw up trying to get inside."

"Of course, I do. I have been fixing our communicators like you so politely *ordered* me to do, which led me to my pod. I was on the way to retrieve yours when the humans found it first. Why Warxhal insisted on that ridiculous propulsion sequence after an emergency release is beyond my comprehension. Took me forever to track it down. Where are you now?"

"Seconds from being taken from the wet ooze. They tried using a machine to electrocute me and killed thousands of creatures instead. Pavil, you should have heard their screams. These fucking humans are soulless."

Pavil's anger stirs through our connection. "Tell me they suffered. Tell me you ripped off their heads."

"I did, but it has cost me."

"Your female will understand. Where is she?"

Pressure sings across my skin as a ligature of some sort is wrapped around my neck and I am yanked through the wet ooze toward several male voices. Even in a semi-conscious state I cannot ignore my bodies response to my suffocation.

"Good night, he's a big motherfucker. Get him in the boat so we can tie him up. Last thing we need is for him to wake up," a rough human voice says.

Something hard scrapes against my suit as they pull me over the side of their craft, finally releasing whatever they tied around my neck to get me there.

As a reflex, I suck in a deep breath, trying to replenish my oxygen, and the craft jostles as several of them jump back. "Holy, shit. He's moving. Branson, stun him! We need to make sure this fuck stays asleep."

I brace for the shock, but Pavil cannot. The bond that connects us allows us to share everything, and our combined pain echoes in the recesses of my mind. Once the impulse stops, my brother's anger explodes.

"Where. Are. You?" he grinds out.

"Stay where you are. This is temporary. Find my female. She needs you more."

"They are torturing you, brother. You cannot expect me to sit by and let them. I'm going to rip off each of their extremities one by one and—"

"You will not. Find my female. Find my Leigh. Wake the others, and then we will have our revenge."

"Where is she? I cannot believe you left her in the charge of another in my stead."

"I had no choice. I had not heard from you. There is a shelter near here where I left her. Inside are her human friend and her pet beast. The furry creature might be foul but it knows her scent well. Speak to it and beware the human may try to kill you." Red hot pain slices across my chest once more, and I fight to remain focused. "Leave. Break our connection. You do not need to feel this. Find her. Now."

Outrage spills across our bond, and Pavil's silence speaks volumes. "I will stay with you, brother—share your pain for as long as I can remain at full strength. We have been together since conception, and I will not leave you now."

As the final impulse ceases, a strange pain explodes in the back of my head and my mate connection screams. My Leigh. Something has happened to her...

A RUSH of cold liquid splashes onto my face, and I am ripped from a slumber so deep, I cannot muster more than a slight memory of it. Pavil was there in my mind, stoking the fires of my irritation as always, but I cannot remember what was said and discussed. I only hope it was enough for him to find my Leigh.

Something hard and unforgiving is clasped around my wrists, abdomen, and ankles and my feet barely touch the floor.

"Ah, so he is alive. How wonderful." A foul scent saturates my nose, and I immediately recognize it as the same one from the lab where my Leigh was assaulted. This is the male responsible for so much pain. "Greetings and welcome to Earth—"

I lash out at him, trying to rip off his arrogant face, but the binds restrict my reach, and he remains untouched. Chained. They have me bound like a beast set to be butchered. As I open my eyes to meet his gaze, he stumbles back and strokes the long piece of cloth wrapped around his neck. "Ungrateful savage..."

Her jerks his chin at another male waiting by the metal wall, and a loud crackle winds to life just before some sort of prod is violently jammed into my back. The scent of burnt flesh fills the air, and the human laughs. "Again," he calls out. "I want to make sure he understands who's in charge."

My shoulder, then my upper back. Both hurt. Not like the pain I experienced in the wet ooze, but without my full suit, the sensation lingers, and I lower my head to combat the pounding in my skull.

The silver-haired male strides forward again, excitement reddening his cheeks. He enjoys this—inflicting pain. Human or not, beings like him cannot be allowed to live.

Agony sings along my scalp as the male with the prod jerks me up by the back of my hair, nearly ripping it from the roots, Blood spurts from his nose and mouth when I rear back and headbutt him. Cocky prick. I may be conserving energy, but I am far from helpless. As expected, he crumples to the ground.

"Got a little too close there, Brando. Go take care of that. Send someone else in."

As soon as the bleeding male limps through the metal building's open door and I am left alone with this...Elgin, he begins to pace just outside of my reach. "You are magnificently different, I'll give you that. I don't care much for the gray skin, but you'll photograph brilliantly.

"We will have to wait until the wounds heal—nothing personal, but we're going to be taking samples of your skin and things like that. I need all the data I can get. It's only a matter of time before Sterling finds out Leigh didn't really steal his money. But now that I have you...everything else will fall away. I'm going to have my moment, and you're going to give it to me." He laughs and claps his hands. "I can see it now. Your ship on display and you in a cage, giving us the answers we've always wanted about life outside of our planet."

My claws lengthen, and the chains bite into my wrists when I lunge for him again. Piece of lecherous trash. I am going to eviscerate him. Then scoop up the remains so I can do it again.

He whistles. "Touchy, touchy. I guess I would be too if I were captured by a man of my stature. I do wonder what it would feel like to be at the mercy of another."

You will find out soon enough.

"Like right now for instance, I have your ship, and my people are getting ready to tear it apart. You know what happens when I figure out what makes it tick? I'm going to track you back to where you came from, then every fucking person alive will know my name. I bet they even name a planet after me."

He lies. There is no way he has breached my pod. It

answers only to me. Each Revari craft is designed for both shelter and travel and cannot be accessed by any outside force.

Clenching my jaw until my teeth ache, I remain silent while he continues to spew his vile intentions. I desire nothing more than to curse at him and rip the tongue from his filthy mouth, but I do not want to give up the element of surprise. In time, I will feed my need to feel the warmth of his blood, but not yet. If he chooses to see me as a pathetic *savage,* I will let him.

At least my mate is not here to witness this.

Several human males trudge inside the metal container where I am bound and stop several feet away from me. Elgin greets them and fans himself.

"Ah, so we're ready? Good. It's hot as hell in here," he says and the male closest to him nods.

With a tremble in his voice, the male answers. "We've got the ship loaded up and can bring it over at any time. We won't be able to get it in here, obviously. But we can get it close. The motorized track he's attached to should bring him close enough for whatever you need. What exactly do you want us to do?"

"Your job. If you need me to remind you, maybe I should find someone else who knows how to pay attention."

The scent of fear and shame saturates the room. "I know that. I meant, what do you want me to do if he doesn't talk. What if he can't? Or just refuses to? Everything we've done to open it thus far has failed."

"If he won't talk, then make him."

Jacob frowns. "How? What do you expect me to do? Torture it out of him? I'm an electrical engineer. That's insane."

"No, what's insane is the amount of money you and your family will have to pay back if you get fired. Or didn't you forget my company supports you? I'll be back shortly. Get the job done, or someone else will."

CHAPTER NINETEEN

Leigh

The smell of wet sand fills my nose a second before a wave of pressure slams against my skull with the force of a sledgehammer. In time with my pulse, the pain hits me in waves and, for a second, I'm on the cusp of passing out again.

No, Leigh. Keep it together.

Still too nauseous to open my eyes, I press a hand to the source of the agony near the top of my head to find my hair crusted with dried blood.

Son of a bitch. Joseph really did hit me.

My lids are heavy when I force them open, and my eyes protest the brightness of the sun peeking through the flaps of whatever tent they shoved me in. I can't afford to give into the pain. I have to get up. Have to figure out what the hell I'm going to do.

There are voices all around me, most of them male and gruff, so for a moment, I listen and try to gauge my surroundings. I'm on the beach given the sand smashed against my cheek where they left me lying on the ground. And guarded, judging by the flash of black fatigues peeking through the tent flap.

I wonder how long I'll have before someone comes back in?

Not willing to take any chances, I push myself to my knees, ignoring the ache in my back, and crawl over to the closest canvas wall. Most of the time, these emergency tents are just staked down and you can crawl underneath the edges...

The brief sense of hope I have dies out when neither the metal frame of the tent nor its thick material give. Wait. Can I dig?

The sand's still wet from the recent storms, making it easier to scoop out big chunks, and the more handfuls I rush to displace, the harder the pressure in my head pulses. Waves of dizziness force me to rest my head against the tent wall but I don't stop.

I don't care how bad the pain is, I'm getting out of here and I'm going to find Saxon.

Light peeks in once I've dug down deep enough, and I drop to one shoulder to look out. I can't see much, mostly because I can't contort my body at the right angle, but what little I can see is clear.

It's now or never. On hands and knees, I dig down as far as I can and shove my head through the opening I've made. Pain sings along my scalp as my hair catches, and it brings tears to my eyes.

Fuck, that hurts.

Crawling on my elbows, I squeeze my hips under the frame, and something snags on the back pocket of my pants. The skin on my elbows chafes against the rough sand, and the tip of what I'm guessing is a screw digs into my butt cheek as I try to force myself through.

Seriously? I can't catch a break...

After several more attempts, the fabric tears, releasing its hold on me, and with one last twist, I manage to free my legs.

My pants are completely torn, exposing the entire left side of my ass, and there's blood welling on my skin where the screw tore into it.

Awesome. Just what I needed. I guess if I'm going to save myself, I might as well do it with my ass out. *Said no one ever.*

More voices filter through the air, including from the guy at the front of the tent, and I have no idea how he hasn't heard me. Once I manage to stand up, I rest against the canvas to catch my breath.

Risking a quick glance, I scan the beach, trying to take in everything, and I'm drawn to a big shipping container at the opposite end.

Could Saxon be in there? Out in the open like this?

It doesn't seem very smart. I've seen how dangerous he is, but Elgin and the others haven't. Could they really be that dumb?

And if he is over there, what the hell are they doing to him to keep him contained?

My gut clenches, and I swallow my panic before it can erupt. No. I'm not going to think about that right now. I might be half naked, but I'm an educated bitch and I refuse to turn into a puddle of goo under pressure. I can't. I need a plan.

I can't go back to Anya's. Chances are she won't even be there after what happened in the woods. With how close we were to her place, there's no way Elgin's guys haven't already found it.

And Binky...

Hopefully, she's sunning herself somewhere like a total brat, completely clueless to what's going on, and I can find her after all of this is over. After wiping the sweat from my brow, a wave of dizziness hits hard, and I have to brace my full weight on the tent.

The middle of the structure shudders beneath my hand before buckling, and I go down hard on my elbow. Pain sings across my palm where a piece of hard plastic used to stabilize the frame jabs into my thumb.

Gritting my teeth, I rip it out, and by the time I look up, there's a gun in my face.

The burly soldier laughs and nudges the edge of the collapsed tent off my legs. "Well, looky here, someone just got caught with her pants down."

Pavil

My communicator vibrates, indicating the corrective code I sent through our shared system have reached Cyfer and Ajax. Their pods will reset and their own communicators will realign and deliver the *wake the fuck up and get up here now* declaration I recorded. The malfunction took too long to spot, but once I figured out it was all related to whatever time glitch the great black hole sent us through, I reversed and restarted the timers our system relies on.

Find my female. Find my Leigh.

My brother's words echo in my mind. The human filth who participated in his capture are crawling everywhere—their stink muddling the light female scent I'm following. If it were up to me, I'd slaughter them all.

My brother has taken to our training like a fucking monk who's devoted himself to a life meant for worship. He holds true to the pillars of conservation and respect like a youngling to its mother's breast, and it's infuriating.

He is the light to my dark, and without that counterbalance, neither of us would survive.

We would not be in this mess if I had been allowed to act. These humans...these puny excuses for living things have pushed him. They have made him something to hunt for sport, and if it were up to me, their heads would be on spikes.

Well, no. Realistically speaking I wouldn't use spikes. Those are hard to come by. But a sharp branch up the asshole would suffice.

They have tortured him. Electrocuted him and yet, he still requests I hold steady rather than pay back his suffering and my own a thousand-fold. If not for his female, this entire village would be burned to the ground for what they've done.

The strength of his connection to his mate flows steadily through my veins, urging me forward. As his twin, the duty to protect her falls to me if he is incapacitated. He is meant to complete her. In his stead, I am meant to save her life and keep her safe. I feel all the strength of their bond with none of its weaknesses.

I share his immense respect for this planet, but these shitbags deserve to die.

His mate's scent calls to me as if it were my own. At least, I'm assuming it's hers, and even though I don't know where it's taking me, I know if I follow, I'll find her without question. I can feel the memory of her presence and I cannot ignore its call. Also, it doesn't hurt that she smells like ripe fruit and I haven't eaten all day. I'm hungry. My stomach is leading just as much as my nose.

At least, it's not my cock. Wouldn't that just be awkward.

Several heavy-footed males comb the trees. Their efforts are abysmal, and if I desired, I could gut them where they stand. None of them even bother to look more than three strides in front of them. How in all the worlds did these buffoons manage to best my brother?

He may carry a bleeding heart devotion to protecting life above all else, save for his mate, but even then, some of these males have spent more time scratching their asses than searching for threats.

Poor human females.

Crouching low to the ground, I inhale once more, trying to sift through the many scents, when the brush stirs to my right. My claws extend, prepared to defend myself if necessary, when a furry creature no larger than a good shit hops out and begins to rub itself on me.

"Tiny creature, I have no use for—" The furry beast winds herself between my legs, making the most obnoxious promises of sexual fulfillment. Saxon failed to mention this creature was in heat. Its aroma is an odd mixture of enticing and bland. I was right about the scent I believed to be Saxon's mate. It lingers on her fur as a result of their continued contact. But what's this? I inhale once more, dodging the female parts the little beast attempts to offer me. Something bolder clings to her. Another scent enticing enough to make my mouth water.

"No matter how many times you offer it, I guarantee it wouldn't fit. Just the tip would split you in half. Now, stop that. It's unbecoming of a female. Not to mention physically impossible."

The furry beast shows no shame as she stretches out to bathe in the heat of this planet's star and reveals herself to me. "What? No, you can't try. Where is your keeper? Did you see what happened to her? My brother has been captured and I need to locate her so that I can keep her away from the human dickheads who took him." With a loud howl, she jumps onto a nearby branch and swats at me.

"No, I'm not lying. Saxon's been taken. There are two of us

and no, neither are willing to satisfy your eh...needs." She cocks her head and lifts her tail trying to...I don't know? Entice me? "Yes, I was told to look for you and no, I won't change my mind. But I will agree to the scratching you request, and before you ask, no. I won't be scratching there."

Accepting my terms, the furry creature describes in very few words how she watched Saxon's mate encounter another male.

"There's nothing more you know? Spit it out. You're holding back."

Flopping back onto the ground at my feet, she peeks up at me. Son of a Anglesian prostitute, she's going to blackmail me. Withhold information until I agree to take her with me so that she can see Saxon is safe for herself. Saucy little minx might be a shit, but I like her style. It's much like my own. Fearless with a certain level of annoying.

"Fine. You can come. Wait, what do you mean they took her?"

The hair raises on her back as my claws lengthen. "Show me. Show me where she fell. But stay back, tiny creature, because once I scent her blood, everything around me is going to die."

CHAPTER TWENTY

Saxon

A loud thud echoes through the metal chamber when I free myself from the human soldier's grip and fling him into the wall opposite me. First, they attempted to draw my blood and take samples. Those males ended up in shreds. Second, they decided to inject me with multiple medications in an attempt to subdue me.

So far, those have not worked in their favor either and, despite my restraints, I have been able to protect myself.

"Grab his hand! Just grab his fucking hand and slap it on there!" Elgin commands, pointing to my pod. He's desperate to get inside, yet unwilling to do the work himself. Sweat drips from his brow, and he kicks a chair across the room in a fit of rage. "It's not that hard! He's in chains."

Jacob throws down the controller in his hand. "Then do it yourself! I'm sick of this shit. We've been at it for nearly an hour just trying to get close enough to grab him, and he kicks our asses every time! We're scientists. Not rodeo clowns. My contribution to science shouldn't require getting my face smashed in."

The two soldiers nearest Elgin exchange a glance, surprise widening their eyes. The largest of the two slaps a hand on Jacob's back and pulls him away.

"Boss, he's right. We have him. He's enough for now. The big guys in the States will figure the rest out. We don't need to get in his ship."

"Levowitz, if I wanted your opinion, I'd fucking ask for it," Elgin yells, charging up to the male who dared to speak. "He isn't enough. I want them both and I don't care if you have to carve the answers out of him, I'm going to get them!

"Leigh made me look like a complete fool when she sank the Nautilus right in front of my colleagues—people with more money and reach than you could even wrap your simple little brain around. Sterling already blames me for her stealing his money, some of the committee even think it's me! I need something big to earn back my seat at the table and this is my fucking ticket there."

The male called Levowitz shakes his head. "Look at him. He's not going to tell you anything or walk over and do what you want. We don't even know if he speaks English. You found a fucking alien. Isn't that enough recognition?"

Elgin jerks his chin to the males standing outside the door of the metal container and it creaks open. "This one needs to disappear."

"What the hell? You're serious?" Levowitz asks as he gets dragged away. "You can't do this, asshole. You're not God."

"You're right. I'm more powerful." The speaking device in his hand rings out and he answers—his twisted frown transforming into a grin. "Get him out of here and bring me someone else who wants to make some money. This thing will talk. We just need to give it the right motivation."

Leigh

"If you don't quit smacking me in the side of the head with that gun, I'm going to kick you in the nuts first chance I get."

My knees buckle as the soldier who dragged me out of the sand kicks the back of my legs, and I go down, hard. Fuck. Note to self. Don't talk crap when the dude holding you at gun point's standing right behind you.

"Get up and shut up."

I throw up my hands after he roughly yanks me to my feet, thankful I had I time to shove the plastic shard I'd managed to keep down into my pocket. "Sorry, sorry. I'm not used to being pushed around."

He purses his lips then shoves me forward again. "You don't say."

"Well, I might be a little more cooperative if you'd just tell me where you're taking me. Any chance it's to the ladies room? Because I really need to piss."

"Might as well tell you, I guess. Not like it matters to me one way or another what that little prick wants to do with you. We're going to see Elgin. He's got your boyfriend chained up on the other side of the beach, and things aren't going so well for him. Seems the freak doesn't want to talk."

I turn back and glare at him. "He's not a freak."

"Touchy touchy," he mocks. "You really screwed that thing, huh? What's its dick look like?"

"I know you're not seriously asking me that." But he is. And it's weird as hell. What's with men and their obsession with dicks?

The closer we get to the more populated area of the beach, the more anxiety I have. I'm trying to walk slowly, but every time I drag my feet, he shoves me forward again and it hurts. I need to figure out a plan. I can't let them take me in there with Saxon and use me as leverage to get whatever they want. And that's exactly what they'll do.

As we pass the last dense patch of trees off to our left, I consider all my options. There's only one right now, and it's the best one I've got. "Okay, I was serious before when I said I need to pee. Can you please let me go pop a squat. The last thing I want to be doing when I talk to Elgin is worrying about pissing my pants."

Soldier guy laughs. "You really think I'm going to buy into that shit? What? You think you're going to take off through the woods and escape? Not happening."

"Please? You can watch me if you want. I don't care, but I really have to go."

He eyes me for a second, then lifts the rifle in his hands. "You run, I shoot. I don't give a shit what Elgin says. There's no way I'm taking a chance on you getting away from here and telling the government I'm involved."

"You're from the US, huh? You stationed at the base over on Guam?"

"Stop with the questions, Nancy Drew and take your piss." I start to walk off to the right a bit, and he jerks me back toward him. "I don't want to watch you piss, but I never said I wasn't going to keep an eye on you. Squat here. I'll take a few steps back."

Damn. The petty part of me was really hoping I'd get the chance to pee on his shoe.

The wind on my naked butt feels wrong, and I'm so nervous, I can't squeeze a drop out. Once I yank up my pants, I kick some dirt around, trying to hide the fact I didn't really need to pee and bend down once more to tie my shoe. Or pretend to at least.

"Oh, come on now. That's the best you've got?" He stomps over. "There's no use in delaying the inevitable. Get up."

"He's going to kill me."

"Better you than me, blondie. I'm trying to get paid, not *disappeared*."

"Aw, you're afraid of him?" I ask, throwing in a snort just to see if I can get under his skin.

All traces of humor flee from his brown eyes. "Nah. Not him, but the spooks he has ties to? All the off the books shit he's got his sticky little fingers in? Yeah, those are the people I'm trying to avoid. I've got my own family to worry about, and Elgin plays dirty."

How did I never know this? I've spent forever working for Daxx Corp. Sure, I knew Elgin was a creep, but I didn't know he was a criminal mastermind. Seems almost comical to think of him that way. Especially since I spent our entire work relationship thinking he was an attention-hungry tool.

"You don't want to be here do you?"

I never noticed before, mostly because I've been too busy trying to figure out how not to die, but the dude looks exhausted and uncomfortable. Maybe, he isn't the heartless bastard I first assumed he was. Maybe, just maybe, I can talk him into letting me go.

It's worth a try...

"Would you? None of us wanted to be involved with shit like this. But once you're on his payroll, you get whatever dish you're served. Money's good, but some of the messed up stuff we're expected to do..." he shakes his head and tightens his grip on the gun. "Let's just say it's not for everyone, and if you can't handle it, you get handled. Know what I'm saying? So yeah, I feel bad for you. But is it enough for me to ignore what I'm supposed to do? Hell, no."

The radio attached to his collar starts to go off, and when he turns away, I slip my hand into my pocket and grab the plastic shard. I have no clue what I'm going to do with it, but it's now or never and honestly, I left crazy behind and landed somewhere between desperate and dumbass about ten minutes ago.

The static crackles over the line. "Ten-four. Yeah, she needed to piss. We're on our way. Tell Elgin not to get his panties in a twist," he replies.

"Hurry up. He's in a mood," a curt voice says in reply.

The soldier kicks the ground and laughs in a condescending way. "In a mood? Of course he is. He's moodier than a bitch in heat." He disconnects his ear piece and takes a swig of the water bottle from his back pocket. "Seriously, *get up*. Don't make me rub your face in it."

The sharp edge of the plastic cuts into my hand, and a thousand thoughts barrel through my mind. What am I going to do with it? Jab him in the neck? Sure, he's a jarhead mindlessly following orders and he's threatened to kill me more than once, but something about shredding his carotid isn't sitting right. This guy is about to turn me into Elgin, but I still can't stomach the thought of killing him so violently.

I can't do it. There has to be something else. Letting the plastic fall back into my pocket, I use a pile of broken discarded branches to push myself up and wrap my hand around the thickest limb in the bunch. Gnarled and knotted, it's firm and not as decayed as the others. The small burst of courage comes out of nowhere and before I can think too much about it, I grip the piece of worn wood and come up swinging.

Shielding my face with both arms, I pant for a few seconds before peeking between my fingers.

Holy hell, I did it. He's laid out on his back, blood trickling from a gash on his forehead. He must have been looking away when I stood up. But why?

Maybe because even with your pants up, your ass is still half out. See he wasn't a complete piece of trash.

The gun is right beside him, but his hand's less than two inches away. If I can get it I'll have something to protect myself with. Well, that is if I can figure out how to shoot it, but how hard can it be?

Determined not to be like the cliché girl in horror movies, I tip toe toward him, careful not to make a lot of noise, and crouch down. The thick strap attached to the weapon is slung over his shoulder, but if I can pull it just right...

As my fingers brush against the hard woven fabric, he flinches and sucks in a deep breath. I bite my lip hard, trying to silence the tiny scream threatening to escape, and if it weren't for the adrenaline pumping through my veins, I probably would have freaked out.

With a trembling hand, I try again. The beat of my heart is roaring in my ears and I'm starting to sweat.

After all of this is over I'm going to need to be medicated.

With a slow exhale, I inch the strap up over his elbow, then his wrist, and soon, all that's left is getting it over his head.

I can do this. I can *so* do this.

If I can manage to lift his head without waking him, I'm home free. I can go save Saxon in a blaze of glory and finally tell Elgin to suck it. Or something like that. At this point, I'll settle for not getting blown up or captured again.

All right, Leigh. It's now or never.

As I'm trying to psych myself up to try one last time, the leaves rustle behind me. Before I have the chance to turn, something smacks into me, hard, and I'm ripped off my feet and tackled to the ground.

Clawing at the hands wrapped around my waist, I roll out of their grip. A strangled gasp tears from my throat and I lunge forward, wrapping my arms around him.

"Saxon?" I croak as my dehydrated eyes fail to muster tears. "They took you. I swear they did. How are you—"

"Look again, female," he says, and it's only after I pull back do I notice a litter of scars splayed out against his chest and the gold cuffs on his ears. He's not my Saxon. But he looks a hell of a lot like him, so much so I could swear he's his—

"Pavil?"

"Ah, so he did tell you about me. What did he say?"

"That you were a pain in the ass. He left out the part where you're his twin."

He tilts his head side to side. "Not the most pleasant introduction, but not far off from the truth."

A jolt of pain sings across my back where my shoulder jarred during my not so graceful landing. "Fuck, that hurts. Did you really have to tackle me?"

"Tackle you? I was saving you. You may thank me now."

Hold up, just one second...

"You didn't save me. I knocked that big dude out before you even showed up."

Pavil narrows his eyes and looks between me and the guy I left unconscious on the ground. "Yes, but he was on the brink of awareness. If you had stimulated him anymore, he would have you pinned down by now. Again, you're welcome, Leigh."

"You couldn't have known that, but whatever, I'll thank you anyway."

He smiles and puffs out his chest like he's really something. "I was concerned when the sexual fur maiden reported your capture. I'm beyond pleased I was able to find you so quickly. And to think my brother doubted me," he scoffs.

Sexual fur maiden? Oh!

"Are you telling me that my cat told you what happened to me? And what's that about Saxon? Have you spoken with him again? Is he okay?"

"She did. She's hiding just over there. Waiting for news of my brother. You know she really has quite the obsession with him, and me as well. The creatures on this planet are so strange. The humans are even worse. The males here are completely inept."

"Pavil..."

"I mean, seriously. I could have slaughtered more than of them with ease."

"Answer my fucking question! Is he okay?" Something shorts out in my brain, and I don't mean to yell, but how unconcerned he seems makes me want to strangle him. What is he even blabbering on about? And why is he so relaxed when his brother's probably strung up somewhere having God knows what done to him?

Pavil throws his hands up, his long black claws gleaming in the sunlight. "By the stars, he said you were tough, but I had no idea. You will make an excellent addition to our collective." I narrow my eyes and start to sound off on him again, but he interrupts. "He lives. In fact, from what I can smell, they are holding him right over there." He gestures toward far end of the beach and the modified shipping container I was drawn to earlier.

"So, they haven't hurt him yet?" I ask, swallowing the lump that's currently set up shop in my throat.

"He has not been subjected to anything he can't handle. You should have heard the nonsensical filth coming out of his mouth while he was unconscious. Nothing chaps his ass like being bested. I should know, I do it often."

"Not from what I've heard. He's made it pretty clear you're the one who always ends up on his back."

He laughs and claps his hands. "Look at you! Defending him. You are going to be even more pleasant than I expected.

Perhaps this terrible planet will offer me an equally impressive mate."

"I'll always defend him. No matter what it costs me. "

Expecting him to make another remark about how inept humans are, I look up to find him staring at me without a trace of humor on his face. Rather than joke, he gets up and helps me to my feet.

"On Revaris, twin births are uncommon and highly desired. For us, protecting those we care for is of the utmost importance and, for a twin, the meaning of this goes deeper than the usual bond. You fought for my brother, Leigh. I will protect you as if you are my own...with my very last breath." His eyes flicker with mischief. "Without all the mating benefits and fun stuff."

"Wow. That turned quickly."

He shrugs and takes my hand. "From my hand to his, female. You will be protected. Now let's go get my brother."

"We need a plan. And that gun." I jerk my chin toward the guy still passed out on the ground. Without word, Pavil walks over and removes the gun, punching the guy in the face for good measure. His nose crunches, and blood starts to well at the bottom of his nostrils.

"Come. These Earthling pricks have been allowed to breathe for too long."

CHAPTER TWENTY-ONE

Saxon

Hot sticky air clings to my skin, threatening to suffocate me. At first, the humans used a machine to circulate the air, making the cramped space they've strung me up in more bearable, but now? They have turned it off in response to my lack of cooperation, and the temperature has risen at least fifteen degrees.

It is fucking hot, and the longer I remain here, the angrier I get. I've tried to break the chains, but with how they have suspended me, I am unable to do so. At least, not until my full strength has returned. I am healing, but every time they suspect I have recovered, they shock me again with their weapons, leaving me back where I started—pissed and waiting for Pavil to do what was asked of him.

If I die like this because he is somewhere jerking off...

I miss my mate and I despise not knowing if she is okay. I swear if those vile humans lay a finger on her... No. I cannot think like that and allow my rage to control my thoughts. I only have one other option and I will not use it unless my situation is dire.

I will trust that Pavil has found my Leigh and is keeping her safe.

Heavy boots scuff against the metal floor as one of the armed human soldiers jabs another electrical prod against my side. Pain ricochets across my chest and down my arm. They figured out quickly that shocking the less dense areas of my suit produces more pain.

"What the fuck's taking so long? You should be done by now." The two males in the room jump, one nearly knocking over his tray of supplies. "This piece of shit is scheduled for transport in less than two hours. We need everything complete then."

"Where's he going?" Jacob asks, panic tightening his voice. As expected, he has still failed to open my travel pod.

"That's above your pay grade, techie. Just do your fuckin' job and get it open. You," he points to the male designated to extract my life blood, "get your head out of your ass and fill those tubes."

"Every time we manage to wear him down and hold him still long enough to try to draw blood, whatever that black material he has on him breaks the needles," he responds, then removes his gloves and sits back in a chair. "I don't know what else to do."

The soldier points to the discarded gloves and snarls, "Pick those back up and figure it out."

"There's nothing to figure out. We can't get past the suit. Mr. Wind is just going to have to accept that it's not going to happen."

The scents of anger and fear permeate the room. "What did you just say?" the soldier asks.

Jacob cringes. "We'll figure it out. Just tell him to give us more time."

"You have ten minutes. Find a solution out or he won't be the only one getting shipped off somewhere when the transport crew arrives."

As soon as he leaves, Jacob scrubs his hands down his face. "Pack up all your needles and stuff, Riz. We're getting out of here."

The male called Riz jumps to his feet. "Are you insane? Lower your voice! We aren't getting out of anything. Daxx Corp has people all over this beach. If you run, you're going to get an Elgin-sized rocket launcher shoved down your throat."

"What other option do we have? His ship won't open, he won't speak, and you aren't getting samples any time soon. They're going to take us somewhere and shoot us in the head, or lock us up where we'll never see the light of day. I should have known better." With trembling hands, Jacob throws his things in a small bag near his worktable and glares at me. "Why can't you just cooperate? Don't you get it? You're going to get us killed."

No, your mouth is what is going to get you killed.

Trying to relieve the throb of the chain cutting into my chest, I shift. The movement of the manacle wrapped around my wrist activates my communicator, and a loud message blares in Revari. *"Wake up, assholes. Hostile planet. Malfunctioning pod. Saxon's been taken. Full mission take down necessary. Use force. Watch your dicks on the way up, it's miserable down there."*

Ha! Pavil did it! The joy I feel at knowing my brethren will arrive soon is snuffed out by the excitement flashing in Jacob's eyes. "Call the hired gun back in here. I've got an idea."

"What? No way, man. He gives me the evil eye every time he comes in. What do you want him for anyway?"

Pulling out a large barb and a set of cables from his bag, the wiry male swallows hard. "Tell him to bring as many guys as he can. We're going to need to unchain one arm and hold him down."

Fuck. This is going to hurt.

Leigh

My muscles burn with the pace that Pavil's set, but I push myself to keep up with him. Choosing to travel through the trees rather than meet Elgin's soldiers head on like he wanted to do, we stop half a mile away to survey what's happening.

The hollow ache that's been slowly chipping away at my heart has worsened the closer we get to the shipping container, and the armor lining my upper half throbs. They've hurt him. Not constantly, but every so often. When they do, I can feel the surge of electricity they send through his body all the way to my toes.

Hold on, babe. I'm coming...

"Do you think you can get us in there?" I ask Pavil as he climbs up a tree monkey-style to get a better look.

"Without question. You will have to allow me to carry you though. It is the only way we can travel fast enough to avoid detection." Pavil looks down at me with a grin. "Do not worry, I—"

The hint of mischief in his smile disappears, and his skin pales.

"Pavil? What's wrong?"

For a moment he says nothing, only stands frozen in place balancing on a limb. His eyes cloud over, and his back contorts. Just as his body shudders, a loud roar in the distance sends my heart plummeting. And then the pain starts. Unforgiving hot lances of pain consume me, raking across my chest and into my back.

Saxon!

Pavil crashes to the ground and starts to seize, grasping at his wrist. A cold sweat breaks out on my neck as I race toward him. No matter how many times I say his name or shake him, he remains unseeing—his face contorted like someone's raking him across hot coals.

My vision blurs with tears as I fight through the pain, and after trying to shake Pavil into consciousness I realize what's wrong. He feels Saxon's pain the same strength as my mate does.

What I'm feeling is only a small slice of his suffering. Hit with another sharp pain, a wild ferocity burns somewhere deep inside me. Erupting like a volcano, liquid hot desperation and a will to live bubbles inside my veins, and then I'm moving.

Pumping my arms so fast they burn, I run through the trees toward Saxon. His growls rip through the relative calm of the waves, and as I come to the edge of the beach, I see the soldiers outside pushing all the non-critical personnel further down away from his container.

With the gun in my hand, I run as fast as I can, kicking the sand up behind me.

Two soldiers fly from the doors—tumbling onto the sand, and two more barrel through to get into the action. It's not until I have my gun pointed at everyone inside the makeshift holding cell that I realize what I've done. Panting in short, clipped breaths, I hold back the tears welling in my eyes.

"Get *off* of him." The words come out strangled and meek, their true strength masked by fear and my need to protect my mate. He's strung up by his left wrist with another chain holding him in place. Six guys in black fatigues are fighting to hold his free arm down while some asshole tries to cut the communicator from his wrist.

"I said stop!" I yell, finally catching their attention and giving Saxon a chance to buck them off of him. His arm falls limply to his side, almost as if they've dislocated or broken it. Green blood oozes down his wrist, and burn marks cover his skin.

I can hardly see past his injuries. It's shocking what humans are really capable of doing. No. It's disgusting and unbelievably cruel.

"Get away from him and against the wall."

Saxon roars and pulls at his chains the second he sees me. There's something primal in his eyes, a violence to their depths I've never seen before. "*Mu Xitall...*"

If not for the group of armed mercenaries in front of me, I might melt into a puddle of goo. I've missed him so much.

"Whoa there little lady, don't do anything stupid now," one of the guys says, lifting his hands in the air. He still hasn't gotten up against the wall. None of them have. "Put that down, and we'll talk."

"Do not speak to her," Saxon growls, and every head in the room turns.

"Ha! Told you motherfuckers he could speak English. Jamie, you owe me fifty bucks."

One of the other men—Jamie, I'm guessing— moves his hand, and I swing the gun to my right, aiming straight at him. "Seriously? Stop moving or I'll shoot your dick off."

"Big words for such a small girl," he mutters. "Why don't you do like Rekker said, sweetheart, put that gun down, and bring that creamy white ass of yours over here?"

Sweetheart? This motherfucker...

Ignoring him, I meet Saxon's gaze. "I'm getting you out of here. Just hold on. If any of these pricks move, I'll shoot them, I swear. I won't let them do this to you anymore. Wait, why are you hanging your head down like that?" I kick the nearest soldier's boot. "What did you do?" Saxon shakes his head and lifts it again.

Jamie laughs. "We might have injected him with some meds. Okay, we injected him with a shitload."

My pulse kicks up, and my vision narrows. He thinks this is funny? That shooting my man up with a bunch of chemicals not even knowing what they'll do to him is a joke? The gun goes off before I even realize I've squeezed the trigger, and surprisingly, it hits Jamie right in the shoulder.

"You bitch!" he yells as he crumples to the side with the force of the impact, and all the other guys in the room go for their weapons.

"Put your hands where I can see them or I'll shoot you, too." I kick Rekker's gun away from where he laid it on the ground. "Give me the keys."

"Or what? You going to shoot me, too?" Rekker asks with so much condescension I might do it just for fun.

"Do you really want to find out? Now, get me the keys to his chains. I want him out. Now."

Rekker shakes his head and shrugs. "No can do. We unchain him, we die."

"Yeah?" I ask, waving the rifle in my hands. "And what do you think will happen to you if you don't do what I say?"

He lunges faster than I can react and grabs the barrel of the gun, jerking it out of my hands. "Nothing. I knew the second you fired off that shot you had no clue what you were doing. Now," he slaps me on my exposed butt cheek and jerks his chin toward the wall. "You get over there, and we'll see just how tough this freak is after I shove a gun down your throat."

"You dare touch her," Saxon grinds out between gritted teeth.

The tension in the room shifts and Saxon changes—pushed so far past the limits of his tightly bound control, he lets go of whatever's been holding him back and gives in. To what, I don't know. But the shift looks to be at the cellular level.

Black droplets ooze down his face and swirl together to create some kind of war paint, and the veins of his neck swell. His claws lengthen, and the torn flesh still holding the communicator in place tightens, then repairs itself.

A cold chill runs down my spine when his gaze connects with mine and he whispers, "*Run.*"

So, I do.

The snap of chains is the last thing I hear as I take off, heading for the trees. The wind is so strong it takes my breath away, but even it can't hide their screams. I stop after only a few minutes and turn around, desperate to see what's happening.

Blood. There's so much blood. Even from a short distance, it runs like a river out of the shipping container. The sand is littered with various body parts. Saxon emerges, covered in a blanket of red so thick it's all I can see and starts toward me.

He might look like the devil himself, but holy shit, if there aren't a million and one nasty things I want to do to him.

There's time for that later, Leigh. You know, when you're not on the verge of dying.

"Don't look. He wouldn't want you to see him like that. He swore once never to invoke the Risha'ri. They must have really pissed him off." Pavil stumbles a little, his skin noticeably paler. "Wait until he has regained control."

"Are you insane? I'm never letting him out of my sight again. And wait, why do you look so terrible?"

His lips press into a thin line, and for once he actually looks affected. "Twin bond. I feel his pain and, in extreme situations, he can take from me, and I from him. I bet you can guess which way it went this time."

"So, that's how he broke the chains?"

He nods, then sways again. After steadying Pavil, I swivel my head to find Saxon. Two groups of black-clad men are headed straight for us, but Saxon's only focused on me.

More soldiers. More of Elgin's people. They must have heard the gunshot. The only people still on this part of the beach were inside that room with us and none of them still have their heads attached.

Rishawaki—or whatever the hell it's called—be damned. I'm going to warn my alien whether Pavil wants me to or not.

"You're more exhausting than he is," Pavil calls out as I slip away and run toward Saxon. Not bothering to stop, I launch myself into his arms and hug him like my life depends on it.

His lips are warm against mine, their taste inspiring the most embarrassing waves of emotion. "I was so worried," I manage in between demanding kisses.

"I am here," he says, attacking my lips once again. His breath is hot against my hair as he buries his nose and breathes me in. "By the stars, I have missed you."

"I thought I lost you," I whisper, "I was so scared and I had no clue how to work that stupid gun. And they had you chained up, and you looked so bad, and oh, fuck. I'm mumbling. There are more of them coming. We need to move now."

"You were wild and fierce and your distraction saved my life. We can only call on the Risha'ri when pushed to the extremes. The pathway to borrow doesn't open until instincts demand it. Until my body does. Your presence," he kisses me and tightens our embrace, "as always, inspires the extreme. Now tell me. Why are you exposed?"

Warmth blooms on my cheeks. "Ah, the whole ass out thing? I tore my pants digging under the tent they held me in."

"I thought someone had...tried to *hurt* you."

"Oh, hell no. Nothing like that."

He lets out an exhausted chuckle then tucks my head under his chin. "And as for your warning. Yes, I know there are more of them on the way. This battle will not be pleasant," he warns, then looks to Pavil. "The others?"

Pavil taps the communicator on his wrist a few times. "They are securing their pods and will be here shortly. What is it you have planned, brother?"

"An Injic'an formation would counteract their weapons and allow me to activate my pod while keeping her safe."

"Hell yes!" Pavil lifts up on his toes and jerks his thumb toward the trees. "Just keep Cyfer and Ajax away from there. They're both thickheaded during battle. The humans put down several metal traps with teeth under the brush."

"What the hell? We were in those trees and you never said anything. If I'd have run through there to get here, I would have stepped on one!"

Saxon growls at Pavil as he shrugs his shoulders. "I was planning to carry you. I just didn't get that far."

"Now, I see why Saxon wants to smack you all the time."

Crossing his arms like a pouting child, Pavil kicks the sand. "Great, now there are two of you."

"So, what about after that?" I ask, anxious to get away from here and somewhere safe. "We just hold them off until we can all get in our pods? There have to be like fifty of them coming this way."

Pavil smiles. His skin already holds more color and the black marks on Saxon's face are gone. "Do not fear, Leigh. Your humans had a slight advantage before. But lucky for us both, my brother's determination to conserve life expired the moment those soldiers touched you. Alone, those of Revaris are strong, but together? There is nothing we cannot do."

Almost like it's a movie, the clouds roll in above us and

thunder claps. The rain starts to fall, washing the remnants of death from Saxon, revealing the male I've come to love.

Saxon and Pavil grasp each other's arms and, as they do, the black of their armor ignites into neon green. The longer they remain connected, the stronger the light grows, and by the time Elgin's men are close enough to hear, I have to shield my eyes from its intensity.

Releasing each other's forearms, they slide their hands down to meet—the neon light crackling between them—then pull apart, leaving a web of glowing energy flowing between them. They slam their untethered fists together, igniting those too, and a shield-like projection spiderwebs in front of them.

Elgin's men start calling out orders, and despite knowing what Saxon and Pavil can do, fear floods me. Saxon pushes me behind him, right in the middle of the web of energy, and I squeak in shock. My hair stands on end, my skin tingles, and once I'm inside, the sound softens almost like I'm in a cocoon. "Lift your feet and let it seal. Nothing will penetrate it, save for the air you require to breathe. It will not break unless my brother and I both fall. Hold on, this is going to get messy." Bullets start peppering the sand less than a foot away and Saxon calls out, "Pavil, right!"

I don't have time to think. I tuck my feet to my chest without question and watch in both horror and amazement as Saxon and Pavil project the energy from their hands and drop everyone close enough to reach. We're flanked on all sides, and as they close in, bullet after bullet freeze outside the protective shield and fall to the ground.

Whatever this is, it's amazing. Pliable enough for them to fight, yet even when they move farther apart and engage the soldiers in hand to hand combat, they remain tethered, and I'm unaffected.

Fighting back to back, with me between them, Saxon and

Pavil continue to mow down entire groups of Elgin's men until all of a sudden, those not directly engaging us back off and start running in the opposite direction.

"What's happening?" I yell. Saxon throws one final energy burst at the soldier charging him, burning a hole right through the guy's chest, and whirls around. I turn, squinting to see what he's looking at but, whatever it is must be too far off for me to see.

"*Insiastic!*" he calls to Pavil, who runs back toward him. They clasp hands, pressing in on me and the energy shell a second before the sand around us explodes. Smoke clouds my vision and it burns the back of my throat. It's everywhere. I can't see—or breathe.

Why is it so strong?

Reaching out, all I can feel is the energy shield around me —its rubbery electric shell tingling against my fingertips—when a morose realization hits me. Saxon said nothing but air could get in. Does that mean I can't get out!

My pulse skyrockets, and my lungs burn as I suck in deep gulps of air, but it's not enough. I'm going to suffocate if I can't get out of here. Banging my elbows against the shell hard enough to send them rocketing back at me does nothing. "Saxon! Pavil! Let me out. Let me out!" I scream.

Another big boom vibrates the inside of the shield, and then another and there's more smoke. Pain flashes across my chest where Saxon's armor is, and something animalistic kicks in. I have to get out, but I can't see anything.

No. No. No. This can't be happening. I can't die like this.

Clawing at the walls does nothing, and my vision begins to narrow. I sway, resting against the energized wall, suddenly exhausted, when a clawed hand reaches in and drags me out.

A wall of smoky air hits me, and I gasp as I'm thrown to the sand. The world tilts, and I jerk up, trying to get my bearings and find Saxon. Pavil's lying beside me panting, green blood dripping from a cut on his head. I rush over and slap my hand over the wound. Bullets hit just a few feet away, so I abandon pressing on the cut, grab his ankles, and pull him back toward the water.

"What's happening? Where's Saxon?" I ask, still coughing and panting. My tongue feels swollen and keeps sticking to the top of my mouth, making it hard to get the words out.

Pavil holds up a single claw and points to my right. Saxon. Less than twenty feet away fighting off the soldiers trying to rush us. "I wouldn't go that way if I were you. Every time I attempt to move that direction, they fire off another one of those damn bombs."

"Bombs?" I rise up to see what he's talking about. Elgin stands next to two guys with big weapons balanced on their shoulders. "Where the hell did they get rocket launchers?"

"This is your planet, female. You tell me," Pavil says dryly, then rolls onto to his knees with a dramatic groan. He stands and dusts off his pants, glaring at Elgin. "No offense, but I really hate humans."

"None taken. So, do I."

Ripping off the bottom corner of my shirt, I try to give it to Pavil, but his wound's already stopped bleeding. "Benefit of being a twin. I heal faster in your presence—as does my brother."

Saxon's still fighting anyone who tries to come near us, but as the smoke continues to clear, I can see others approaching from the opposite direction.

"Leigh? Come out, come out wherever you are," Elgin taunts over some sort of loudspeaker. "Are you ready to stop hiding, or do I need to shoot at you some more?"

"I really want to kill that guy," Pavil says, shoving me

behind him. The light on his communicator brightens under its protective flap of skin.

"Join the club."

The loudspeaker squawks again in the distance. "Still not feeling chatty, are we? All right, then. Maybe this will change your mind." The guys next to Elgin start loading the rocket launchers and Pavil pushes me back several steps in response.

Eyeing the growing group of black camo-clad guys getting in position to our left, he whispers, "Can you run?"

"I can try."

"When I say, run for the water. Understand me? Don't go for Saxon. Don't turn back to look for me. Just do it."

"But what about—"

Pavil groans. "For once in your life, listen. I'll take care of it. Just do as I say."

"I don't know if I can do that."

The soldiers to our left start to move, and Pavil turns back to look at me. "You can, or there's a good chance we will miss our opportunity to leave. Did you notice the other humans closing in on us to our left? This is taking too long. Every moment we spend out here, we risk more exposure. We only have a small window. Don't fuck it up. Go to the water when I ask."

"This is your last chance, Leigh," Elgin calls out. Saxon lets out a roar as he drops another guy, but he's tiring. Moving slower with each soldier he bests. So is Pavil. Something has to give.

"Fine," I manage, nearly choking on my instinct to refuse.

Pavil growls and scrapes his claws down his suit. The neon green lights flicker in and out. "Damn it," he curses. "Sorry about this. Instincts need a little motivation."

"Ow!" Without warning, Pavil pokes my hand hard enough to draw blood and shoves it in his face. He inhales, then shakes his head and scrapes his claws down his arms again. The light flares, and he manipulates it into a shield in front of us.

A voice streams through his communicator saying a bunch of stuff I don't understand and Elgin calls out to us once more.

"Get ready," Pavil hisses.

The guys to our left are getting closer, some even near the water, and my gut clenches. They could easily reach me that far away from him.

"You're sure?" I ask again, just to make sure. Fuck, this whole trusting someone with your life thing is hard.

Blood continues to well on my hand. The wind changes direction, and Saxon roars. "*Mu Xitall!*"

"So predictable," Pavil murmurs. "Go."

"What? Now? What about Saxon?"

"Of course, now. He'll follow. Go!" he yells, just as the first rocket whizzes through the air. I don't make it three feet before it explodes against Pavil's shield in a deafening blast. I push harder and faster toward the water.

One foot after the other. Simple stuff, right?

The sound of footsteps to my right has my heart jackhammering in my chest. "Stop right there!"

Fuck. Fuck. Fuck. This was a terrible idea.

My side burns, and I still can't breathe from the smoke and damn, if I survive this I swear I'll do some cardio.

Like a ray of intergalactic sunshine, three silver egg-like shapes pop up out of the water and hover just over the surface. The hope they inspire spurs me on. Pods. They must have found Saxon's. We're finally going to get out of here. *Faster!*

I can see the soldiers in my periphery, closing in, but I don't stop. I'm nearly there, toes just inches from the water, when two hulking gray shadows rise from the sea and lunge for the soldiers at my back.

Holy shit. One of them is even bigger than Saxon.

Red stains the surf, and when the two Revari males flank me, I get the distinct feeling everything's going to be okay. "I am Cyfer. You are Saxon's female?" the first asks. His long black hair is woven around his neck in an intricate pattern, and half of his ear is missing.

"I am. Can you help him?"

His laugh is loud and gritty. "Your kind...they have bones that break, yes?"

"Yeah, why?" I ask, heart still in my throat. Saxon's managed to push back the group of six pressing down on him and the pile of bodies at his feet is so large he's having to step over them to fight.

The second Revari male throws Cyfer a metallic tube. He taps it to the communicator at his wrist and it expands, forming a giant energy scythe. "A whole lot of shit is about to die." He laughs again, and I swear the water vibrates around him with its strength. "Ajax, spike me!"

Ajax and Cyfer do the same weird forearm grab Saxon and Pavil did, and his scythe glows brighter.

"Don't worry, female. This won't take long." Cyfer lets out a roar loud enough to vibrate my ear drums, and then he's gone. Hopping person to person, he destroys everything in his path.

"It's about time you assholes showed up," Pavil yells, voice strained with exertion. Another rocket explodes against his shield, and the energy flickers in and out. "It won't last much longer. Saxon, get your ass to your mate."

"Leigh! Your beasts can't keep this up forever! Give up and bring them to me or I'll make sure they die!" Elgin shouts.

Tired of his shit, I cup my hands around my mouth. "In case you haven't noticed, asshole, you're losing."

Several more rockets slam into Pavil's shield, and he curses at us over his shoulder. "Can you not do that? I'm getting really fucking tired. Saxon," he yells. "Let Cyfer finish them."

Not needing to be told twice, Cyfer zooms over, toppling the crowd of five huddled around Saxon like bowling pins.

Wait, did he just giggle?

"*Mu Xitall,*" Saxon whispers as he wraps me in his arms. "Are you whole?" He looks me over, feeling me for wounds. "Forgive me for not being there when you were removed from the shield. I had little choice."

"Shut up," I murmur, kissing him hard.

"I will do whatever you wish as long as you do that every day for the rest of my existence," he whispers against my lips. Damn, I love him.

"Well, fuck. If I would have known that was what it took to get you to give, I would have swapped spit with you a long time ago," Ajax says, his long black mohawk blowing in the wind.

Almost as if he's noticing him for the first time, Saxon smiles at his friend and they press the sides of their heads together. "I fear it would not have the same effect. It is good to see you, Ajax."

"Likewise, friend."

"I hope you're having a really beautiful reunion back there while I'm struggling to stay on my feet. Can someone go kill that asshole already so we can leave?" Pavil yells as his heels slide back after yet another blast.

"On it," Cyfer calls out, still knee deep in the other wave of Elgin's guys. They've got to run out soon. This is a tiny island. I mean, where the hell are they even coming from?

Ajax jerks his head toward the pods. "Get her strapped in. We can take it from here."

I shake my head. "No, we can't. Not yet, not without Binky."

"Saxon, I can't hold this much longer. It's at less than ten percent," Pavil grinds out between clenched teeth, his voice barely carrying over the gunfire. Just then another hard blast hits his shield, and Pavil flies back, landing hard on the packed, wet sand. Ajax rushes to pull him up. "Okay, maybe less than ten percent."

Even near death he jokes.

As soon as he's on his feet, I'm at his side. "Where is she? Where's Bink?"

"Who?"

"My cat. You said she was in the trees. I can't leave without her."

Pavil glares at Saxon, who's holding me protectively. "She's serious, isn't she?"

There's no way I'm leaving her. I know she's a cat, but she's the only family I have and I'm not abandoning her wondering where I've gone or why I left her. It's not fair and she deserves more.

The brothers lock gazes, and when the whirl of bullets start again, Saxon throws me over his shoulder and heads for the pods.

"No! Put me down. Please, please don't make me leave her," I beg, beating my fists against his back. "Please, I swear I'll go get her myself."

"Pavil will retrieve her."

The spray stings my eyes, and no matter how hard I try to wiggle out of his hold, his arms are like granite. Completely unmovable.

"Swear to me. Swear to me right now, he's going to get her. If you're lying, I'll never forgive you."

Flipping me around so I face him, he cups my face. " I will never lie to you, *Mu Xitall*. Nor will I allow you to die. You are my mate. My universe. I am taking you home. Pavil will bring the furry overlord. He gave me his word he would deliver her before we seal the door."

CHAPTER TWENTY-TWO

Pavil

Ignoring my aching muscles, I push toward the line of trees where I left the furry creature Leigh calls Bink. I think the fact she asked me to run through a battlefield to find it is absurd, but if there is one thing I have learned in my short existence, it's that all females are.

And I would do anything to have one of my own.

Using the bodies that Cyfer has piled up as a shield, I sprint past him and the humans he still battles into the trees far enough away from where Elgin's men are still trying to blow a hole in my brother to avoid detection.

At this point I'm so tired and hungry, I don't really give a shit. If one more fucking human tries to shoot me, I'm going to rip out its throat.

Tracking the creature by its scent, I'm led into an area laden with traps. I don't step on them because I'm not a fucking idiot, but I have to wonder why they have all been left there.

The furry creature's scent isn't the only one that lingers here. Several males. And Elgin.

"Looking for this?"

Whirling around, I extend my claws, ready to tear out the tube that gives him that awful voice, when I notice the furry creature dangling from his hands. Not to mention the tiny silver wire strung around its neck.

Well, fuck. This complicates things.

"Release the creature to me."

Elgin laughs and pulls out a small black weapon. More projectiles? Don't these humans have any other types? They're slow and clunky and, quite frankly, hurt like hell to dig out.

"No chance. I don't know why you left that bitch, especially after you fought so hard to hide from me, but I'm not letting you go twice."

Twice? Ah, the human mistakes me for my brother. This could work in my favor. If I want it to. Do I even care? Should I just slit his throat and hope he doesn't injure the creature before he drops dead or is it worth the risk? Saxon's female seemed particularly attached to the hideous thing.

I shake my head, tilting it to the side for effect. I've seen other alien species do it to appear intimidating. Normally, I would not have to, but this human clearly doesn't recognize a predator when he sees one.

"Fine, then. I'll kill the little bitch and take you with me anyway." He grabs a black box off a clip on his pants and begins to speak into it. "All available units report to my location. I got the bastard."

My claws lengthen, and the scent of Elgin's fear surrounds us. He's terrified of me, yet he won't release the stupid thing. "Give me the creature and you will not be harmed. Much."

The sound of more projectiles flying toward Saxon and the

other males on the beach stifles the tiny bit of amusement I feel knowing he's afraid, and annoyance takes its place.

"Perhaps, my understanding of your language is skewed. Give me the fucking creature, or I'll slit your throat. How about that?"

"I'd rather die than go to jail. The only way to redeem myself in Sterling's eyes is to bring him something worth more than what I've taken. Facing my colleagues without you and your ship isn't an option. I've got nothing to lose."

"Very well."

The human swallows hard, his finger squeezing the trigger. I don't move. I don't need to. The pitiful projectiles cannot pierce my suit. So I use the split second to slice through the metal wire around the creature's neck. Out of nowhere, a tiny being smashes into me and knocks me to the ground.

Her scent hits me, wrapping around more than just my nose, and as she stands and cocks a weapon of her own, my dick nearly jumps out of my pants.

Holy Harcraftian tit rings. She's hot.

A long silver braid hangs down her back like some kind of tail, and she holds the gun steady.

Elgin sneers. "Ah, I was wondering when I'd see you. What is it you're calling yourself now? Anya? You might consider making another choice. You have no idea what I can do to you—"

Without word, she fires her weapon right between his eyes. "Asshole," she mutters, then plucks the furry creature from the ground as he collapses in a lifeless heap.

Need like I've never known thickens my blood, forcing it all the way to my cock and I can't think. Who is this majestic creature in front of me?

"You must be the twin," she says. But again, I can't speak. For the first time in my existence, I have no clue what to say, and it's fucking wonderful. "Right. Okay, then. Get the cat to Leigh. She'll be heartbroken without her. And when she asks how you found her, tell her... Ah, hell. That'll be too hard. Just leave me out of the story, okay? She's had enough to deal with."

I stand there dumbfounded, taking this *cat* creature without question and watch as she turns away, then tosses a quick glance over her shoulder at me. "Seriously, I see all your people out there. She won't leave without Binky. Go. That prick might be dead, but he's got a hell of a lot of people on this island on his payroll. Not to mention, by now, the entire government knows what he says he has, so either get the fuck out or start killing people."

"Female, why did you save me?" The single question is all I can manage. I mean, technically she didn't, but she thought she did and that's all that matters.

She pulls down her face shield and smiles. "I really have no clue. Take care and make sure he treats her right."

The urge to follow after her consumes me, setting every part of me on fire. My instincts demand I answer them.

Mate. I have found you.

Grabbing the furry creature, I take off for the beach, completely rejuvenated with the news. I should have known her scent. Tiny wisps of it clung to the creature and to Saxon's mate, but I dismissed them.

Fire licks across my shoulder as I catch not one, but two projectiles. I cannot slow down. I need to get back to this... Anya. To find her. To follow her around and convince her that she belongs with me every day until she cannot stand to be away from me.

Or hopefully, something simpler. I'll take what I can get.

Leigh begins to weep when she sees me bounding toward her. "I don't get it. I thought you'd be pleased," I say, handing the cat over.

Saxon glares at me. "She is. It is a chemical reaction in humans when they are overwhelmed with joy. And upset. And quite possibly other things..."

"Oh."

Saxon slices his wrist, spreading the required life blood on the pod's exterior to open its door, and it responds as I hoped. He immediately frowns. "Brother, this is...not my pod."

"Of course, it is," I say, not meeting his gaze.

"Perhaps it has been too long since I last saw it." He narrows his eyes, searching the interior while setting his mate inside. "Relax, *Mu Xitall*. Lean back against the life foam. It will feel strange at first. We do not have time for it to conform as it normally would."

"Thank you, Pavil," Leigh says, sniffling with whatever strange emotion human females exhibit.

"Of course. And do not worry about the human leech. He's dead."

Her eyes brighten. "Really? He's gone?"

"He is. There is nothing left for you to fear. Go and be with my brother. Revaris will treat you well."

Cyfer sprints toward us from the beach, covered in human blood. "Well, this was fun. Let's not do it again."

The humans have stopped shooting and are now staring at us from the shore. My female...she has gone back to hide in the trees. I need find her.

Saxon steps into his pod and shakes his head. "This does not look right, Pavil. What have you done?"

"Be well, brother. I will join you shortly."

He wraps his hands around the door hinge, preventing it from closing. "What do you mean 'shortly'? What are you up to?" Slicing a claw across my own hand, I slap it on the pod's exterior and smile. "No."

With that single word, I know what he means. He doesn't

need to say more, but knowing my brother, he will. "You cannot give me your pod. You do not need to do this."

"Yours was never functional, brother. Not yet, anyway. Do not worry about me. The risk is not too great with what remains for me here. Take your female and go home. Tell mother and father I will see them soon. I have a mate to catch."

Slamming the door closed, I watch to ensure the exterior seals completely before I turn and run back to the beach in search of the one meant for me.

CHAPTER TWENTY-THREE

Leigh

The sickly wet feeling of this foam is making me want to crawl out of my skin. It's in my ears, and all I can hear is the dull hum of my heartbeat. Binky's here, purring against my chest, and Saxon's hitting a bunch of buttons. He still hasn't said anything. At least, I don't think he has.

I try to reach out to comfort him, but my arms are already molded into the foam, so all I can do is talk and hope I can hear him.

"Are you okay?" I ask, but rather than answer, he continues to do whatever he's doing, then turns himself around in the tiny space so that he's facing me and his back's against the pod door.

He hits another button on his communicator and the foam cradling me in place spreads around him, too. Once it covers his ears and everything behind him, he starts to speak.

"I am fine, *Mu Xitall*. Getting better every second with you near me."

"What was all that with your brother? I couldn't hear but it looked intense."

"It is of no consequence. Do not trouble yourself. Tell me, are you okay?"

I try to shake my head but its stuck in place, so I smile instead. "I'm terrified. Worried about what happens next. Elgin's men are still out there. What if they figure out how to find us again? How long is this going to take? Will I feel anything? What's going to happen?"

He reaches out and presses his fingers to my lips. "That filth may not have died by my hand, but your life—our life together—is more important than seeking vengeance. Where we are going, your kind cannot follow. We are safe here. We will go to sleep, just like this." He moves closer a bit, leaving the foam that had already cradled to him to follow after. He presses his forehead against mine, leaving just enough space for Binky to move. Normally, I wouldn't want someone so close to me, but I need his touch, and Saxon doesn't have to tell me he needs me too.

We've been through so much in such a short period of time. And this is the first moment we've spent together where no one's trying to kill us. Well, except for maybe space. But at this point, there's not a damn thing I can do about that.

Three sets of needles rise from the foam, and I tense. "What are those? Tell me they're not going inside me."

"Just here and here." He points to my wrist, then his. "And thanks to Pavil's recent modifications, one for the furry overlord as well. They will assist us with sleeping and keep us fed through our journey."

With a slight pinch, the sharp barb pierces my skin and a cool wetness begins to flow through me. It feels gross at first, then a few seconds later, the odd sensation disappears entirely.

Like being in an elevator, I can sense movement around us

as we take off, but I can't muster the energy to be worried. Whatever juice is flowing through me veins is like Valium on steroids.

Saxon grabs my hand and squeezes tight. Despite being inside and safe from Elgin's men, my heart's still racing.

"Don't let go, okay? I'm worried about waking up and forgetting where I am."

The depths of his sunshine eyes swirl as he meets my gaze. "I will never let you go, *Mu Xitall*. And as I have many times before and will continue to do, I will carry you through your dreams."

CHAPTER TWENTY-FOUR

Saxon

"Wake, my child. Wake..."

The sweet sound of my mother's voice whispers in my mind. The exterior of my pod is responding to her presence as it was created to do. It is customary for the first greeting once returning home be from those who created you. Our capsules recognize their life blood just like they recognize ours.

The cold chill of the serum coursing through my veins recedes, leaving a slight throb as they warm. My consciousness flares, my eyes adjusting to the darkness of my pod as the injection needle slides from my wrist and the foam releases me.

A warmth settles deep in my chest, comforting me in a way I have never known. I have succeeded in my life's mission. Leigh is here, with me, and I am home.

Like some sort of gift from the spirits, my female lies sleeping, her face a wash of relaxation. Her golden locks have grown, now trailing down her back. The worry and fear that etched her face so often before are gone, and all that remains is smooth, unmarred skin, fresh from the nutrients the pod system provides.

She is exquisite. And she is mine.

Before waking her, I check the furry overlord to ensure the tiny creature has survived. The complex tasks of sustaining such delicate life forms have not been tested before and the last thing I want to do is wake Leigh up to find the overlord did not survive our journey here.

She would be devastated, and after all she has suffered, would not recover from the loss.

Gently, I remove the tube feeding my mate's beloved creature and she too stirs, blinking awake. Relief washes over me, and despite the wretched beast's decidedly unsavory behavior, I am almost pleased to hear her continue her lust-ridden advances.

Taking in Leigh's beauty once more, I gently remove the injection tube from her wrist and draw my own blood to press against the tiny wound. The gesture will go unseen, but recognition does not matter. I want my female to start her life here anew with no wounds to remind her of her past trauma.

Her skin feels clammy against my own as I hold her upright, supporting her while the foam recedes, and like many other races outside of my own, she remains asleep. The stasis serum affects her differently, and she will wake slower. I have to resist growing anxious during the wait.

As always, my movement triggers the pod's opening sequence, and it scans the environment around us. The hatch releases, and I bring my female against my chest, fully cradling her in my arms, then step out into my mother's embrace.

I have returned and fulfilled my duty as an Exune. Brought honor to my family. But even more than that, found the match to my soul. The female created by the ancient sky spirits for me, and I will never take this gift for granted.

Leigh

"*Zor a et in'askulatian vex tocart,* Saxon," a sweet voice says, her words carrying like music in the wind. I'm so tired I can hardly muster the energy to pay attention but then something soft and warm presses against my bare cheek—his lips, maybe? —and he answers back in the same unknown language. "*Yar as, Mu Jortec. Leigh ut.*"

A slight sting to the back of my neck sends a brief shock of pain down my spine but it's gone before I even have the chance to respond. Saxon whispers in my ear, "Shhh, my everything. Do not fight it. Allow the implant to work."

Implant?

A light breeze rustles my hair, sending the strands flying every which way. I'm surrounded by warmth and the familiar feel of Saxon next to me. It's pleasant wherever we are and it smells of fresh flowers and something else...citrus, maybe?

With my hands tucked up under my chin, I snuggle in Saxon's massive arms and enjoy the light jostle of him carrying me. I don't even care where we're going. There are no bombs going off and I'm not seconds away from having a nervous breakdown.

Wait. Why is everything calm? And where's Binky? Crap, am I dead?

Jerking up with the grace of a wildebeest, I topple backward, nearly falling out of Saxon's arms. An odd inhuman cry tears from me, and I spin my head around trying to figure out what's going on. "Fuck, I am dead aren't I?"

Saxon chuckles. "If you are, I am also Can a dead male do this?" he asks, grabbing my hand and pressing it against his massive erection.

"In my version of heaven they could." Binky's collar jingles, and for the first time, I see her prancing around Saxon's feet. On purple soil. Wait? Purple?

Sitting up as straight as I can without falling, I scan the landscape around us and gasp at its beauty.

A blazing golden sky lit up by two bright red-orange suns staggered on the horizon. Trees with deep blue and forest green leaves are clustered in the distance with the most beautiful flowers I've ever seen.

"Is this..."

"My home, my everything. It is your home, too."

"My everything? Wait. You've never called me that before. You sure this isn't some kind of weird afterlife I've conjured up?"

He presses on the back of my neck, and a mild soreness flares to life. "Your implant is working. My mother met us on arrival and delivered it to me. She is anxious to formally meet you."

So, that's what Mu Xitall means...

My hands immediately go to my insane hair and unwashed face. Not to mention, my ass is still half out. I smack him on the shoulder, and he cocks a brow. "You let her see me like this?"

He nuzzles my nose with his. "It is customary for the Exune and their mates to be greeted by one or both of those who gave them life. My mother came alone today. She is who received our pod and woke me."

"How did she even know to come if you didn't call her?"

He shrugs. "Everything on this planet is automated and requires very little interaction to initiate. Receiving those who have returned is one of the customs we have chosen to nurture and keep intact. Like our destined mate, our return is delivered in a vision to the ones who love us most."

"Did she like me?" I ask, my cheeks warming. I know it's a

stupid question to ask seeing as she hasn't even met me yet, but she saw me and the vain part of me wants to know what she thinks.

"She may have spoken a few words…"

The curve to his lips makes me smile. I like this version of Saxon. Teasing and joking. All of our relationship so far has been doom and gloom, and now that we're here, I feel like I'm going to see a whole new side of him.

"Like what?"

Saxon whistles, and within seconds, a hovercraft of sorts zooms around the corner and lands. I follow his gaze as its door opens without words. "Whoa, how'd you do that?"

Gently releasing me into the seat, he steps away and climbs in the other side. It's weird, like something out of an *Star Trek* episode. There are no handles, no buttons, no screens. Just some kind of shiny black metal lining the inside, two bucket chairs, and bags full of weapons in the back area.

Saxon looks back, and his cheeks darken. Wait. Is he blushing? "I am sorry. I did not think to clean it out before I left. I was so excited to find you."

He licks his lips. A nervous habit, maybe? And he's so damn cute, I can't contain myself. We're both gross, and Binky's in the back of the car glaring at me, but my hormones don't care. His brows shoot up in surprise when I climb into his lap.

"Leigh," he groans as I press my lips to his, but whatever else he says gets lost between hungry strokes of my tongue. His cock's like granite beneath me, and with every twist of my hips, he brings me closer to coming. He hasn't even gotten my pants off, and I'm ready to explode.

"Touch me," I blurt out, caught in the moment as I drag my hands into his hair and deepen the kiss. "I've never wanted anything or anyone so bad in my life."

Gripping my ass with both hands, Saxon presses down on my hips and angles his own, increasing the friction between us. "More," I demand, increasing my speed to grind on him harder, but it's not enough. I need more.

Saxon reaches beneath me to grab his cock. "You want this?" he asks, running a hand down his length. If I was turned on before, the sight of him stroking himself sends me way past nuclear.

"Yes," I answer, mouth dry. "Do that again." I lean back and watch as he once again runs his hand up and down his cock. He's so big, my core clenches at the reminder of the night we spent together in the hut, and I can't take it.

Attacking his lips once more, I reach past his waistband and grip his cock. It's warm against my palm and already slick with precum.

"You are mine," Saxon growls. A heated moan tears from my throat as he rips open what remains of my pants and yanks them and my panties to the side. With one swift motion, he enters me, and I cry out, completely consumed by him.

My thighs burn as I bounce up and down, matching his every movement. I want and need every inch, every single sensation, and when he bucks his hips, driving himself deeper inside me, I come so hard I nearly pass out.

The car or whatever it is lurches forward right at the end of my last moan, and Saxon climaxes. I try to lift my head as best I can, but the world spins so I give up.

"Is this thing...driving by...itself?" I manage, still trying to catch my breath.

Saxon bucks his hips once more in the aftershock of his orgasm, then tightens his arms around me. "Yes."

"Shouldn't you be controlling it or something?" I ask. There are plenty of windows, but none of them are positioned like the ones on Earth.

"It does not require navigation assistance, only a command to initiate transport." Saxon rubs a thumb across my furrowed brow.

"Are you telling me you were thinking about driving when we were—"

"No," he rushes to answer, then kisses my forehead. "I may or may not have yelled the word *go* in my head when you reached your pleasure point. Perhaps it thought I was speaking to it."

I tilt his chin down so I can see his eyes. Laughter bubbles up despite my best attempts to control it, and I snort. "You're serious aren't you?"

"I like it when you come. I quite enjoy making you feel that way."

"I'm not complaining. That far exceeded anything I ever hoped for from car sex, but shouldn't we know where we are going?"

"It is taking us to my home. There is a celebration in your honor, and you will require clothing." He chuckles and picks up one of the pieces of my shredded pants. "I seem to have been a little overzealous. I apologize for leaving you with so little to wear."

"Stop apologizing. That was so hot. Just thinking about it makes me want to do you all over again." Saxon's pupils widen, and his nostrils flare. "Oh, geeze. Don't even think about it. Put that thing away before you break me. I'm sure I'm already going to walk like I've been riding a horse."

"Horse?" he asks, and I laugh.

"An Earth creature you ride around for transportation. It's not important. Tell me more about this celebration."

CHAPTER TWENTY-FIVE

Saxon

She is beautiful. The length of her yellow hair is braided up into a bun, and she wears the Revari colors—red and gold—around her eyes. Tradition calls for my mother to assist her, but since she requested not to meet Leigh until after my mate had rested from our journey, I had to do my best.

Where females have a delicate touch, my hands are rough and cumbersome, but my Leigh looks ethereal nonetheless.

She chews on her thumb waiting for the procession to begin. She has yet to be revealed to them but once she is, she will understand she has nothing to fear. "So what am I supposed to do again?"

We have discussed this multiple times, but she is convinced she will forget something. She does not understand her existence is a miracle in and of itself, and that is why my people have gathered to welcome her.

No one here will judge her or dare to put her down. She

comes from a world where everything must be proven. Every scrap of respect earned. Here, value is innate.

"You simply walk. All Revari present will act as they are moved to. Some cheer, some stand silently by your side in quiet contemplation. Their reactions will vary, but your task is always the same. Just walk. I will be by your side and, if at any time, you do not wish to continue on, we will leave."

Leigh blows out a breath and straightens. "All right, I'm ready."

I grab her wrist as she starts out the door and intertwine our fingers. "Always together."

"I love you," she whispers.

"And I love you, mate."

With her at my side, we open the door to my dwelling and she stiffens the second she sees the massive crowd waiting for us. I nudge her forward with a hand on her lower back, and as we move closer, the group parts.

Flowers float down from the sky to settle at her feet as my people toss them.

"What does this mean?" she asks under her breath as we walk through a sea of pink.

"Throwing Yu'Kuvu flowers is a sign of gratitude and respect. They are covering your feet to bless the path you have taken. I attended over a hundred of these as a youngling and never have I seen such a display." Tears gather in her eyes, and my need to protect her ignites. "We do not have to continue on if you wish to leave."

"No," she shakes her head. "They're gorgeous. I just wish I knew how to thank them without looking awkward, you know?"

"This moment is yours, my everything. Do with it as you wish."

"There aren't any words big enough to show how much this

means to me. Thank you for bringing me here." She tugs me down as we pause on the makeshift walkway and presses her lips to mine, earning us several loud cheers from the males in the crowd. Her shoulders loosen. "Males... You're all the same, no matter the planet."

Unable to resist the urge to hold her, I wrap my arms around her middle and scent her hair. "I will be anything you wish."

"You're already it." She smiles and tries her best to acknowledge everyone we pass. With the bulk of those who chose to greet her in our wake, we pass under an altar of Ro'tor flowers to find my mother and father waiting for us with none other than our king.

"Is that her? Saxon, she's so beautiful." Leigh says as the bright red headpiece adorning my mother's head comes into view. Males in my culture are expected to remain emotionally unmoved, but the vision of the second most important female in my life just as fulfilled and happy as the first makes maintaining myself difficult.

My father stands by her side and narrows his eyes in warning. King Kizan is to his left. Tightening my jaw, I allow my claws to lengthen and rein in the soft emotions my two females inspire. My mother and father dip in a low bow to King Kizan, showing the appropriate respect, then turn to us.

"It is so good to finally meet you. We have waited for this day for so long. I am Eisa and this," she gestures to my father, "is Vrukai. Welcome home, daughter."

Leigh covers her mouth, then without warning lunges at my mother and pulls her into a full embrace. My mother tightens her arms around my mate and holds her without hesitation. Those remaining close cheer, and King Kizan steps forward.

"Saxon of Revaris, Exune of our people has returned with

his mate!" More cheers and grunts echo through our collective. "Come, shower them with well wishes and enjoy yourselves on this fine occasion!"

"SHE IS WONDERFUL, Saxon. The ancients have surely blessed you." As always, my mother sits neatly, hands tucked at her side as she watches the males tell stories of the times they have bested each other. Although she has engaged the other females and accepted their praise, she has sat alone for the last few moments deep in thought.

My Leigh sits on the steps of the home I secured before I left with the furry overlord in her lap. She looks tired, the hours of gaiety wearing on her. My people do not indulge often, but when they do, the celebrations go well beyond the set of our final sun.

"She is more than I could have hoped for. More than I ever hoped to deserve."

"If only your brother could find an equally impressive female to settle him. His mind is always wandering."

"Do you worry for him? Fear that he has not returned? I know you were hoping the ancients would send us our mates at the same time."

She presses her hand to her heart. "He lives. I still feel him here. You forget you have not been gone that long, my son. Your journey may have felt like an eternity but time has hardly passed here. The marker for your birth has yet to pass. It is you I worry about. You two have never been separated."

"The world we left behind was not a *peaceful* one. I will spare you the details, but perhaps, that is why I am left uneasy in his absence."

"He is a Revari male, is he not? You and your brother are

trained to fight and to protect those who cannot defend themselves. Pavil will find his mate and return to us just as you have. And if he should fail, you have my full permission to search the stars, find him, and kick his ass."

"Mother!" I gasp, unaccustomed to hearing her speak vulgarities. She is a warrior, deadly enough to earn the markings of Revari elite, but she has never shown us anything but unwavering understanding and strength.

"What? You are matured and no longer need me to shelter you from my occasional slip of the tongue."

The furry overlord jumps from Leigh's lap and scurries through the crowd, shouting demands, and my mother narrows her eyes. "How does your mate tolerate this creature?"

I clear my throat, unsure of what to say. Even as a child before being instilled with the Revari code of ethics and swearing my oath, I could not deceive her. "Leigh cannot understand the foul words it speaks."

"And you managed this how? The tiny beast is not exactly quiet about her disdain. Or her desires for...completion."

"I altered her chip. If she knew of the things it says, she would be heartbroken. She loves it. And despite its foul temperament, it loves her, too."

When the wind shifts, scattering the brightly colored flowers lining the ground, my mother catches one and places it in my hand. "You are a good male, Saxon. Go to her. Let her rest her eyes and be done with this night if she wishes. But most of all, love her as your father has loved me, and you will spend the rest of your days with endless happiness."

"With her, it is impossible to feel anything else."

Drawn to her like the pull of a Xisun moon, I make my way toward her and everything else fades away.

"Are you okay?" she asks as I offer a hand and pull her to her feet. The light streaming down from the final setting sun reflects off her eyes in the most intriguing way. Just the sight of her in our traditional dress stirs my desire, and I am painfully aware of my need for her.

"You are here," I whisper. "How could I not be?"

She laughs and tugs me closer by the black chain adorning my uniform. " Since when did you get so smooth? I feel like now that we're not being chased by an army and dodging bombs, we'll have to get to know each other all over again."

I shake my head and angle my hips so she can see what she does to me. "I know you. From the second I felt the connection between us stir me awake, I knew without a doubt you were meant for me. Whether spent in turmoil or sweet relief, an existence with you is all I desire." Her nipples harden underneath the thin material of her U'chai robes, and a hint of her arousal teases me.

"To feel you underneath me, to taste you at first and last light every day the ancient sky spirits see fit to keep me breathing is all I have and will ever dream of. You need not worry, my Leigh—my everything. You are it for me, and I will spend the rest of my life loving you."

Her pupils dilate. "Can we go inside? I'd really hate to attack you out here but if you keep saying shit like that to me, I don't think I'll be able to help myself."

A deep growl rumbles in my chest, and I am throwing her over my shoulder and carrying her up the few steps to our door before she can blink. It opens, responding to my thoughts, and as soon she is on my bed, I stop and take in her image. Cheeks reddened with arousal, swollen lips and hooded eyes so blue she puts her planet's sky to shame.

"Do you know how exquisite you are?" I ask, peeling back the thin layers of cloth keeping the flush of her skin from me. She parts her thighs, welcoming me in, and with soft strokes of my tongue I drink her in.

"Saxon," she moans, tangling her hands in my hair. " Please...don't...stop..."

She whimpers once more, then arches her back as I score my teeth along her sensitive nub. "We have forever mate, and I do not plan on stopping any time soon."

EPILOGUE

Leigh

The rides into the major cities still make me nervous. It doesn't matter than I've been living in the Revaris countryside close to a year or that I've ridden in roans nearly a hundred times, I just can't get used to them. Autonomous cars have their own special place in hell.

There's something about giving up all control that doesn't sit well. Probably because I worked for a megalomaniac who attempted to kidnap and murder me.

Fun times.

Usually Saxon's there to distract me, but this time I went solo. His mother came to me this morning right as he left to train with the other males and said the ancients came to her in a dream. Pavil is returning, and for some reason, I needed to bring a Roshini cloth soft enough to keep a Zoros egg from breaking.

I guess it's a good thing she gave me a list because I have no idea what the hell a Zoros is and I've never seen a Roshini cloth. Yet, here I am. Nearly tripping out of one of those blasted cars with an armful of bags to wait in the small garden I've managed to grow. Saxon's mother should be here any moment to pick me up to meet him.

The waxy leaves of my Yu'Kuvu flowers have finally started to peek through the purple soil, and in just another few days, they should be in full bloom. The keyword here is *should*. The plant life here, like all the other living things on this planet, has a mind of its own and is far more sentient than what grows on Earth.

If you happen to choose a seed that doesn't like you, it just won't grow. Yeah, living here has been quite an adjustment.

The days are longer, the nights shorter, and their year is comprised of over four-hundred Earth days. Don't even get me started on how they don't use toilet paper.

The communicator Saxon created for me buzzes around my neck, alerting me to a foreign presence near our house. The device is a little heavy and sometimes gets in the way, but it was either this or having one surgically implanted in my arm.

After watching Elgin's men try to dig it out of Saxon, I just couldn't do it. I try my best to push thoughts of what happened away, but there's so much good mixed in with all the terrible we experienced. We've only grown closer, fallen deeper in love, and I swear, if anyone ever tries to take him away from me again, I'll rip their face off before they even get close.

Eisa's roan comes around the corner, and I stand to dust off my pants. The heel of my shoe rustles the Yu'Kuvu bud, and I drop to my knees. "Shit, I'm sorry. Don't get mad. I swear, I'll sing to you later."

Up again, carefully this time, I head over and slide in beside Saxon's mother.

"By the ancient sky spirits, you look lovely. Have you told him?" she asks, her deep citrine eyes sparkling with excitement.

"No. He's still in the training circles with Deg and the other warriors."

She claps her hands, then quickly checks her hair. "Wonderful. He will be so pleased. This is the longest they have been apart, and I cannot wait for them to be reunited!"

"Oh, here." I grab the bags of stuff she sent me into the city for and hand them over. "Are you going to tell me what all of this is for?"

"That part...is *your* surprise, my daughter. And it will be a big one."

"Oh, fun! Do we know when he's going to be here? How does that work anyway? Do the dreams give you an exact time or..."

She smiles and pats my leg gently. "The ancients are wonderfully mischievous. They send images only. Some are mere flashes, and they are left up to the receiver for interpretation. The suns were low in the sky. Much like they are now. Call him to our location but tell him nothing. It should be any moment now."

After meeting Saxon, you'd never know his mother and the rest of the Revari females are festive. The males are the polar opposite—cold and at times, unforgiving. They focus solely on the protection and defense of their home. But their decidedly curvier counterparts?

They find joy in absolutely everything.

Makes me feel a bit out of sorts at times, still dragging around so much baggage. It's getting better, and with Saxon's steadfast reassurance, most days I don't even think about the events that brought us together.

Trying to practice maintaining the connection between my chip and my communicator, I close my eyes and focus on the buzz in the back of my head. Letting go of the urge to do, rather than think, is harder than I expected. Everything here is designed to sync with your chip and operate hands free.

Saxon answers instantly. "My everything, are you all right? You do not normally call upon me while I am working."

"Yeah, but I need you and I can't exactly tell you why."

A deep growl carries over the communicator. "Are you harmed? Has the furry overlord gotten herself in more trouble? I know you love the cursed creature, but she refuses to keep her distance from the other mated males."

Saxon's mom rolls her eyes, and I try to contain my laugh. He's so protective, and while most of the time I get a kick out of it, I also think it's freaking hot.

"No, nothing like that. I actually left her at home. I just need to show you something, but it has to be now."

"Will you be naked?" he asks in a low voice, and I blush bright red, silently praying his mother didn't hear.

"Is that all you think about?"

He chuckles over the line. "Yes. You *are* all I think about."

Well hell, how can I stay annoyed when he says stuff like that?

"No, I will be fully clothed, but I still expect you to show. The naked part comes after."

"How naked?" he asks almost immediately.

"Like the day I was born."

"Right then. I am leaving now."

I try to get another word in before he severs the connection, but he's already gone. The male is insatiable.

Eisa invites me to join her sitting on the hood of the roan while we wait. Let's hope for both our sakes she doesn't mention the mini-foreplay Saxon tried to start during our call.

"I used to do this as a child on Earth—stare up at the sky and watch the clouds roll by. I can help you if I know what I'm looking for."

"Some things are universal. Saxon and Pavil both used to join me in doing that very same thing while we waited for the Exune of the past to return."

"It sounds like he had a really great childhood."

She gives my hand a squeeze. "He did, as do all younglings raised here. Your progeny will be no exception."

Here it comes. The conversation I've been dreading. Saxon and I have been doing it like rabbits, but mother nature still hasn't done her thing. Eisa hasn't said anything, and she's never put pressure on me to get pregnant, but the possibility of not meeting everyone's expectations always hangs in the back of my mind. I can't help but feel like she wants more from me.

A lot of little mores. And I want them, too. And they'll happen when my body is ready for them.

We sit there in comfortable silence, leaving her statement open ended because I have no idea what to say, until a loud boom sends Eisa to her feet. "There. He has arrived." She points to a green streak not far off in the distance.

She's nearly a quarter of a mile away before I can blink, and I rush to catch up with her. I don't even know why they bother to use roans when they can run so damn fast. The females are especially quick.

As I jog toward her, my communicator warms, letting me know Saxon's close. He's going to be so excited. I know he misses his brother. He mentions him all the time, so much so, I had a hard time at first listening to him.

It might sound selfish, but I was pretty messed up emotionally after everything that happened, and once Saxon and I settled into our wonderful new life, all I had was time to think. Think about how I'll never mend my relationship with my sister. About how I left Anya after everything she did for me.

Don't get me wrong, I'm happy. Happier than I've ever

been really, but stuff like that doesn't just float away because your circumstance changes.

Everything I've faced has only made me stronger.

Now that I've graduated to the point of using those feelings rather than trying to run away, it only makes me appreciate Saxon more.

He wakes me every first sun rise with a kiss, and I'm not just talking about my lips. He feeds me, holds me when memories keep me up at night, and most importantly, he never stops wanting me. Wanting to listen, wanting to be around me—it's been a year and we're still just as crazy about each other as we were when we first met.

But for him, there's always been something missing, and his brother coming home is the last piece.

Holy crap, I'm so excited to see him.

His roan comes to a stop near a cluster of trees between his mother and me, so I veer off to meet him. He's bounding toward me before the hover mechanism can disengage. Once I'm in his arms, I nuzzle against the corded muscles of his neck and enjoy the sweat clinging to his skin.

"You got here fast," I say, popping my head back up to kiss him.

He chuckles and gives me one more squeeze before setting me back down. "I had a substantial amount of motivation."

"Yeah? Like what? Getting out of sparring with your father?"

My skin tingles as he runs a claw from my neck to the apex of my thighs and flicks my clit through my pants. "You know what I want. What I always want. Do not pretend you do not know what you do to me."

The bulge in the front of his pants is getting larger by the second, and no matter what my lady bits are telling me, we don't have time for it. "Easy there. I'd hate for your mom to catch sight of your raging hard-on."

His face pales slightly. "She is here?"

"Yep. And that's not all. Come on, pick me up and carry me over to her, I'm slow as shit."

Saxon laughs as he lifts me in his arms. "You are not slow, my everything. You are not as quick as I am because the ancients meant for me to carry you."

I hold up a hand before he takes off. He's going to figure it out in a few feet and I really want to be the one to tell him.

"Wait. I want to say something to you before we go over there. I love you, and I'm so incredibly happy we found each other, but I swear, if you try to move him into our house, I'm letting Binky sleep on the bed."

"Who are you talking about? I do not understand—" He squints, and as soon as he realizes who I'm talking about, his sunshine eyes light up like the Fourth of July, and he starts running.

His mother is the picture of pure joy as she greets us, pulling us both in a hug.

"Pavil," Saxon whispers, a hint of child-like excitement in his voice.

"Would you like to do the honor?" Eisa asks, holding the blade they use to draw the blood necessary to open the pod.

"No, Mother. That honor will always be yours. But I ask that I be excused from all consequences. He deserves to be throttled for what he pulled back on Earth, and I would be remiss if I didn't greet him accordingly."

Eisa shakes her head and smiles. "You two... I will allow it."

Holding the knife between her hands, Eisa says a small prayer then drags the blade across her palm. She smears it across the seamless silver tube and whispers something I can't hear to make a door appear.

"Now, we wait for him to wake." She jumps up and down a little, then kneels and presses her forehead to the ground. "By the ancient sky spirits, thank you for bringing my son home. May you bless him and my new daughter."

A sucking noise brings her to her feet, and Saxon squeezes my hand. The door opens a fraction but rather than Pavil's smirk, we're greeted with a tiny hand.

Eisa sucks in a deep breath and, with trembling hands, opens the pod door wider. Toddling out like she's always belonged there, a little girl no older than two jumps into her arms.

"Wait! Annie, get back in here. Shit, your mother's going to kill me."

The door to the pod swings wide as Pavil tumbles out looking for her. As soon as he sees her safe in his mother's arms, his shoulders relax, and he sighs. "Oh, thank the stars you're here. She's a handful." Eisa, tears in her eyes, is clutching the child like her life depends on it. "Mother, don't cry."

He lumbers over to hug her and she shakes him off, motioning for him to grab the Roshini cloth. Once he does, she wraps it around the little girl's shoulders. "I am not crying. There is something in my eye."

Pavil laughs. "I'm sure there is. My mistake."

"She is so beautiful, Pavil. The ancients themselves could not have made a more perfect youngling."

"That was all her mother's doing. My contribution lasted a mere second."

Saxon snorts as Eisa narrows her eyes. "I see some things have not changed."

"Much to my mate's detriment, no. I still offer a bounty of jokes. Thank the ancient sky spirits, she chose to love me anyway." For the first time, Pavil notices Saxon, and if I'm not mistaken, he too gets a little bleary eyed.

All traces of humor drain from both their faces as they pull each other into a quick embrace. "It has been too long. Nearly two Earth years by my account."

"One by ours," Saxon answers, and the softness to his eyes is replaced by a hardened glare. "And not long enough to forget the foolish sacrifices you made."

Pavil looks to me. "Is he still going on about this?"

"Hasn't stopped since we left," I answer, giving Saxon a wink.

A cacophony of frustrated groans and muffled curses float out of the pod, and my stomach sinks to my toes. I know that voice.

"How is your mate awake?" Saxon asks. "Is she not human? It took Leigh twice as long to rouse when we first arrived."

"Oh, she is. That woman does what she wants, chemistry be damned." He smiles and waggles his eyebrows. "She's a reality bender, Saxon. And she's done more than whip me into shape if you know what I mean."

Eisa grimaces. "He knows what you mean. Unfortunately, we all do. Now bring her out here so I can meet her."

Pavil's gaze connects with mine a second before his mate peeks out of the pod. I run toward my best friend, nearly knocking her over in the process. Before we hit the ground, Pavil and Saxon are there to catch us.

"Anya? How? Why? Wait...you and Pavil?"

Ugh, I know that's not her real name, but I can't stop calling her that.

"Me and Pavil," she says, smiling at her little girl. Eisa sets her down, and she runs for Anya.

"Hey, I'm not that bad. I only had to follow her around for two weeks before she agreed to spend time with me."

"It was closer to three," she says with a smile and leans in for a kiss. "He drove me insane, but I'm glad he did. He brought me out of the hell I was living and gave me Annie. He's the best choice I've made so far. Most days, anyway. I still have moments where I want to backhand him."

"Those are the days when the se—" Anya slaps a hand over his mouth to muffle the rest of the word, "is the best."

"Watch your mouth around Annie."

He throws up his hands. "Sorry, sorry. Seriously, come here and let me hold you. Traveling that far wreaks havoc on your body. I need to make sure you're okay."

She swipes a hand through the air. "I'm fine."

"Why must you be so stubborn?" he asks, arms crossed.

"Why must you insist on coddling me?" she challenges.

Once Anya and Pavil stop bantering back and forth, he introduces her to Eisa and we all get to meet her sweet little girl. With three of them completely exhausted, our reunion is short-lived, and I opt to ride home with Saxon.

Pavil, Anya, and Annie go to Eisa's house to recover before their welcoming since Pavil doesn't yet have a home.

Five minutes into the drive, the reality of Anya's arrival hits me, and I start to cry. I know I missed my sister, but in all honesty, Anya was family the second I met her, even more so than my own blood. The last year has been wonderful, but there's been this weight I've carried around knowing that I left her, and for the first time in a long time it isn't there.

Saxon pulls me over to his side of the roan and into a tight hug. Something tells me I'm not the only one who needed it, because he's clinging to me just as tightly as I am to him.

Pavil coming back means more than just the return of his brother. It means he's one step closer to achieving his dreams of a completed family. A family with me.

And Anya? I can't even describe what her being here means to me.

We spend the entire trip home like that, crushed in each

other's arms. And when we arrive at our little piece of heaven and he carries me inside, an intense feeling of gratitude overtakes me.

This male, this being has given me a life I never thought to ask for.

"I love you," I say, trying to put into words how I feel. It's not enough, but it's the best I can do.

"And I love you, mate."

The bed is soft as he lays me down, and the brightly colored flowers he picked for me on our morning walk shine beautifully in the sunlight.

"These tears," he gently drags the tip of his claw through the wetness gathering on my cheeks, "they are for joy or sorrow?"

"Joy," I say. "Definitely, joy. I just realized today how happy you make me. I always knew, but it's easy for it to become the norm. But to feel like this...to get to wake up to you every morning, I don't think I could ever ask for anything else."

"That is how I feel about you."

I sniffle. "Yeah? You sure you won't get tired of me?"

"Could anyone tire of living? For me, that is what you do, my everything. You give me life. The suns are brighter, my heart beats stronger, even the winds themselves seem to blow harder in your presence, and I will always feel the effects. You are the center of my universe, Leigh. Do not ever forget it."

"Yeah?"

"Yes. Now, kiss me. You made promises of nakedness, and it is time for your debt to be paid."

And so I will. Over and over. For the rest of my life.

THE END

ACKNOWLEDGMENTS

First of all, I couldn't do anything without the unwavering support of my husband and our family. If not for you, I'd still be typing one sentence at a time, then going back later and deleting it. I want to give a huge shout out to my wonderful editor and my team of alpha and beta readers! You guys are the best. Also, I want to thank every person who picks up Saxon and spends a little time in his world. I appreciate each and every one of you.

ABOUT THE AUTHOR

About the Author

Annalise Alexis is a free-spirited mother of three who lives with her husband and kids in the heart of Texas. A huge fan of Firefly, Gilmore Girls, and anything with Jason Momoa, Annalise combines her love of all things sexy and strange by writing in several genres including: science fiction romance and paranormal romance.

Don't forget to join her newsletter here: http://eepurl.com/ga7Vk5 for snippets, sneak peeks, and all the things.

You can also find Annalise's Word Fiend reader group on Facebook here: https://www.facebook.com/groups/1799904083451498/.

Website: http://annalisealexis.com
Instagram: http://bit.ly/2BuiXDV
Facebook: http://bit.ly/2EEUhwr

ALSO BY ANNALISE ALEXIS

Printed in Poland
by Amazon Fulfillment
Poland Sp. z o.o., Wrocław

58618173R00132